bird

atheneum
Atheneum Books for Young Readers
New York London Toronto Sydney New Delhi

bird

Crystal Chan

ATHENEUM BOOKS FOR YOUNG READERS
An imprint of Simon & Schuster Children's Publishing Division
1230 Avenue of the Americas, New York, New York 10020

For information about special discounts for bulk purchases, please contact
Simon & Schuster Special Sales at 1-866-506-1949
or business@simonandschuster.com.

The Simon & Schuster Speakers Bureau can bring authors to your live event. For more information or to book an event, contact the Simon & Schuster Speakers Bureau at 1-866-248-3049 or visit our website at www.simonspeakers.com.

Book design by Debra Sfetsios-Conover
The text for this book is set in Adobe Caslon.
Manufactured in the United States of America
1213 FFG
First Edition
2 4 6 8 10 9 7 5 3 1

Library of Congress Cataloging-in-Publication Data
Chan, Crystal.
Bird / Crystal Chan. — 1st ed.
p. cm
Summary: Twelve-year-old Jewel was born on the day her brother Bird died and lives in a house of silence and secrets, but a new boy in her Iowa town
may help find the answers Jewel wants despite her Jamaican grandfather's
warning that he is a "duppy," a malevolent spirit.
ISBN 978-1-4424-5089-9 (hardcover)
ISBN 978-1-4424-5090-5 (eBook)
[1. Superstition—Fiction. 2. Grief—Fiction. 3. Family problems—Fiction.
4. Selective mutism—Fiction. 5. Racially-mixed people—Fiction.
6. Iowa—Fiction.] I. Title.
PZ7.C359116Bir 2014
[Fic]—dc23 2013002377

To the trees, water, earth, and sky, who give of themselves that I may share my story

—C. C.

CHAPTER ONE

GRANDPA stopped speaking the day he killed my brother, John. His name was John until Grandpa said he looked more like a Bird with the way he kept jumping off things, and the name stuck. Bird's thick, black hair poked out in every direction, just like the head feathers of the blackbirds, Grandpa said, and he bet that one day Bird would fly like one too. Grandpa kept talking like that, and no one paid him much notice until Bird jumped off a cliff, the cliff at the edge of the tallgrass prairie, the cliff that dropped a good couple hundred feet to a dried-up riverbed below. Bird's little blue bath towel was found not far from his body, snagged on a bush, the towel that served as wings. From that day on, Grandpa never spoke another word. Not one.

The day that Bird tried to fly, the grown-ups were out looking for him—all of them except Mom and Granny. That's because that very day, I was born. And no one's ever called me anything except Jewel, though sometimes I wish they had. Mom and Dad always said that I was named Jewel because I'm precious, but sometimes I think it's because my name begins with *J*, just like John's name, and because they miss him and didn't want to give me a normal name like Jenny or Jackie. Because John had a normal name, and now he's dead.

It was my twelfth birthday today, and everyone was supposed to be happy. It was hard to be happy, though, when Grandpa shut himself up in his room for the whole day, like he does every year on my birthday. Mom and Dad made me a cake with vanilla frosting and sprinkles, gave me a present—some socks from the dollar store, but they're cute and all—and the three of us went to the cemetery to visit Bird and Granny. I always watch those movies where kids have big birthday parties with music and party hats and huge presents and even ponies, and I think it would be nice to have a birthday like that. Especially the ponies. Just once. Instead, I've always had to share my special day with the silence behind Grandpa's closed door and the silence at the cemetery and the silence that hangs thick between Mom and Dad's words.

Mom and Dad washed the dishes from my birthday cake and went to bed, but I couldn't go to sleep, just like every year on my birthday, because I kept imagining what Bird was like, what kind of brother he would have been, and what five-year-olds think when they throw themselves off cliffs.

So I did what I often do when I can't sleep: I changed into my jeans and a long-sleeve shirt, put on some bug spray, and crept out of the house and into the star-studded night. There's this huge oak tree just down the road in Mr. McLaren's field, and I often climb that tree as high as I can, and lean my back against its warm, thick trunk. There, I watch the moon arc through the sky and listen to the whirring of the crickets or the rustling of the oak leaves or the hollow calls of the owl.

For a moment, I thought about going to the cliff where my brother flew. But I knew better than to go there at night.

Now, in my small town of Caledonia, Iowa, we have one grocery store with one cashier, named Susie; three churches; our part-time mayor, who works in our town hall, which also serves as the post office; two restaurants that run the same specials, just on different days; and fourteen other businesses. Things here are as stable as the earth, and that's how folks seem to like it. No one's ever told me that going to the cliff should be kept secret, but that's one of the things about adults: The most important rules to keep are the ones they never tell you and the ones they get the angriest about if you break.

I wouldn't tell them I go to the cliff anyway, because adults don't listen to what kids have to say. Not really. If they did, they would actually look at me when I talk, look good and deep and open-like, ready to hear whatever comes out of my mouth, ready for anything. I don't know any adult who's ever looked at me like that, not even my parents. So the good stuff, the real things that I've seen and experienced, like at the cliff—I keep all that to myself. My family doesn't fit in as it is.

Anyway, tonight I was making my way down County Line Road, which still radiated heat, and my tennis shoes were scuffing against the gravel when suddenly I got the feeling that something was wrong. Different. A shiver zipped across my skin. I stopped and looked at my oak tree. The moon was waxing, growing slowly toward its milky whole self, and the tree was glowing and dark at the same time, its arms spread wide like a priest's toward the sky. As I squinted in the silver light, a pit formed in my stomach, and I realized what it was.

Someone was already in my tree.

"Heya," said a voice. It was a boy's voice. I tensed up all over. There's never anyone outside at this time of night, grown-up or kid. Maybe it was a duppy, those Jamaican ghosts that Dad always worried about. Duppies' powers are strongest at night, Dad says, and they often live in trees. You can tell a duppy lives there when a tree's leaves blow around like crazy even though there's not a speck of wind. Or if one of its limbs breaks off for no good reason. If something like that happens there's definitely a duppy in that tree, right there. Duppies can also be tricky and just show up. Like, they can be in your tree when there was never a duppy there before.

But the boy's voice carried long and lonely through the night in a way that I didn't think a duppy's voice could, and each leaf on each limb was perfectly still, frozen in the moonlight. On any normal night I might have just played it safe, turned around, and run back home, but it was my birthday, my special day, and I wasn't going to go running away and let a duppy ruin it. So instead I said, "Hey," back, and I stepped over the shoots of corn, crossing the dry, hard dirt of Mr. McLaren's field. The boy was up on the third limb—the same limb I was meaning to sit on—and his shadowed legs straddled the branch like a horse, swinging back and forth, back and forth.

He was in my tree and I felt kind of stupid, like I didn't know what to do.

"What are you doing out here at this time of night?" he asked me. I peered up but couldn't see his face.

I tried to shrug casually. "I climb my tree sometimes, when I can't sleep."

"Is that true?" He said it surprised, but like he didn't really want an answer, so I didn't give him one. "But it's not your tree, now, is it?" he said.

"It's not yours, either."

The limb creaked, like he was peering down at me. I squirmed a little in the moonlight. "Is too my tree. I'm John. This is my uncle's farm, so it's my tree. I can climb it anytime I want."

I'm sure he said some other things, but my brain stopped after he said *I'm John*.

I must have looked as stupid as I felt, because his voice got a little nicer. "You know, not too many other kids live around here in this middle of nowhere. Especially not many who climb trees at night."

And before I knew it, he was asking me to come up and sit with him, and I was shimmying up the rope that I'd tied and then climbing the warm, tough bark of the tree, hand over hand, legs pushing forever up, until I was sitting on the branch below his. John's face was still dark, as I was craning my neck up into the cool shadows.

But I was sitting in a patch of moonlight, and he got a good look at me. "Hey," he said, "what are you, anyway?" The words were curious, not mean. "You're not from around here."

A little *something* tightened inside me, like it did every time I got this question, but I was used to it. Mostly. "I'm half-Jamaican, a quarter white, and a quarter Mexican," I said.

"Wow," John said. "I didn't know people could turn out like that."

"And I *am* from around here," I said, making sure my voice carried over the crickets. "I was born in the house down the road."

John said, "I'm not trying to insult you or anything. I've just never met someone like you."

I twirled a thick, kinky lock of hair around my finger, then untwirled it. I've learned that it's best to get this conversation out of the way so we can talk about more interesting things. "Well, now you have," I replied. "And my name's Jewel."

He nodded, almost like he already knew that. "Jewel," he said. His voice lingered over the word. "I like that name."

"I don't."

"It's memorable. Like, everyone's going to know they've met a Jewel. But 'John'? Forget it. We're a dime a dozen."

"No, you're not." The words came out too fast, too harsh, too laden with pain I forgot to hide.

John paused in the darkness, on his third limb. "Okay,

maybe a dollar a dozen, then." He spoke carefully now. "But I still think Jewel is nice."

We sat in that tree in the middle of the field under the waxing moon. Suddenly he said, "You know, stars are like jewels. But they don't twinkle like you think. What your eye perceives as twinkling is the light waves refracting through the layers of the atmosphere."

The way he spoke, he sounded like a teacher. A good teacher. Maybe that's why I decided to ask a question, not like in school. "Refracting?" I asked.

"The light bends," he said. "At a lot of different angles, depending on the layers of atmosphere, and that refracting light changes how we perceive the position and size of a star." His voice hung in the space above me. "The only way to see the stars as they truly are is to get above the atmosphere. Into space."

There was no breeze that night, just a thin layer of moist air that hung around us, like the entire earth was listening in.

"I never thought about stars like that."

John laughed, and it was a short, nice laugh. "Just wait until the Perseids show up."

"The what?"

"The Perseids. A huge meteor shower that takes place in August."

I had never seen the Perseids before, or even heard of them, and I said so.

"It's okay," he said. "Most people can't see what's in front of them if they don't know what they're looking for. But once you know what you're looking for, you wonder how you *didn't* see it. Just wait: Once you see the Perseids, you'll see them every year, guaranteed."

"How do you know so much about stars?" I blurted out.

I heard the smile in his voice. "I'm going to be an astronaut when I grow up."

John was so different from the other kids in Caledonia. Most kids around here want to be mechanics or nurses or take over the family business. I almost told him that I was going to be a geologist when I grow up, but I didn't. Instead, I was quiet. If you give up too much of yourself, too fast, then someone can just up and take it away. And a person like me, without too much of my own to start with—well, you need to be careful with what you got.

I don't know how long we sat there, but sitting in that tree felt different this time around. Maybe I was getting too old. Or maybe it was just strange sitting there with someone else.

I climbed down after a while, and he climbed down after me. I saw him for the first time clearly in the moonlight, and it was then that I realized why I couldn't see him all that well before: His skin was dark, dark as the night sky.

"You're McLaren's nephew?" I blurted out. My mouth was too fast for any politeness. Mr. McLaren is as white as white could get.

John smiled, and his teeth shone like tiny rows of moons. "Sure am. I'm adopted. Raised by white people. It's not as bad as it sounds."

I wasn't sure if he was talking about being adopted or being raised by white people, but I nodded as if I understood. He held out his hand, and I took it and shook it, just like the grown-up I was becoming. I was surprised at how firm his grip was, like we were going to conquer the world.

It was the best handshake ever.

But handshake or no handshake, as my shoes crunched against the gravel on my way home, I wondered about how I could meet someone named John on this night. As Dad says, there are no coincidences in life. Which is a fancy way of saying that when things are meant to happen, no matter how mysterious or crazy or impossible, they're going to happen. And I think he's right.

CHAPTER TWO

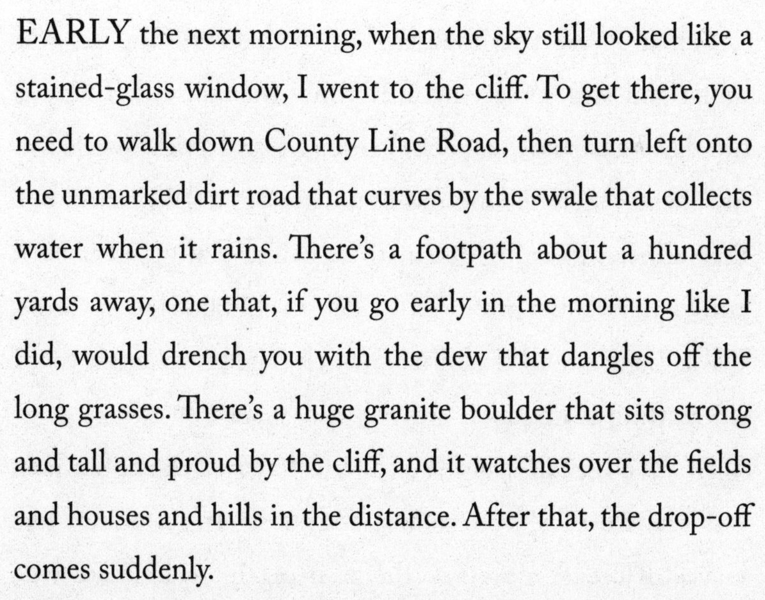

EARLY the next morning, when the sky still looked like a stained-glass window, I went to the cliff. To get there, you need to walk down County Line Road, then turn left onto the unmarked dirt road that curves by the swale that collects water when it rains. There's a footpath about a hundred yards away, one that, if you go early in the morning like I did, would drench you with the dew that dangles off the long grasses. There's a huge granite boulder that sits strong and tall and proud by the cliff, and it watches over the fields and houses and hills in the distance. After that, the drop-off comes suddenly.

I decided not to tell my parents that I'd met a boy named John, and that I found him in a tree. I've long grown used to not telling them really cool things, because they usually don't get excited, anyway. Once, I found this great arrowhead in the backyard, and I ran inside to show it to them, and instead of wondering how old it was or what tribe made it or asking if I ever wanted to be an archaeologist, Mom looked at me sternly and said, "Throw that outside. You know better than to come in here with dirty shoes."

It happens all the time. Something cool happens, and they just block it out. It's as if Bird was the only cool thing that could ever happen, and now that he's gone, nothing else can ever be great or incredible or mysterious.

When I saw the boulder, I slowed down. The air was moist and still. I was the only thing that moved. Today is the day I add another rock, I thought, and pride swirled in my chest. I searched around in the grasses until I found one that wanted to come out of the earth and wiggled it back and forth and dug around the sides until I had it in my arms. It was bigger than the others, which made me happy, too. I was getting stronger.

At the edge of the cliff, beside the massive granite boulder, was a circle of eleven stones. They were large stones, like loaves of bread, eleven of them sitting in a circle so wide I could do cartwheels inside it. I got there, told the eleven there was going to be a new one and they all needed to get along, and arranged them how they wanted to be.

Twelve. Just like me.

Even though it's not good to have favorites, I have to admit that I did. I found my seventh-year stone by accident; I stubbed my toe on it that first summer when I didn't know any better and was wearing flip-flops. I was going to pick it up and put it where it couldn't get hurt when I realized that I had to keep digging around the sides; it was much larger than it looked at first. It also had these strange swirls of pink in it, which I liked.

Or take my tenth-year stone. That one was a gift, really, like the earth heaved it up into my arms, looking nice and new and pretty, with quartz angles jutting out in every direction when I peered at it closely. I couldn't hold it too tightly or I could cut myself, but that's precisely what I liked about it.

My circle sure looked different with the twelfth-year stone there, in a way that made me proud. Outside the circle and down a ways, where the soil got thicker and loamy, was a row of saplings that grew from seeds that I planted last summer and sat with when it rained. On the other side of the circle lay an area of upturned earth.

The middle of the circle was empty.

The sun crept up and over the hills to the east. I paused

at the circle, slipped off my shoes, and stepped inside. The dirt was loose and cool and whispered against my feet. I faced the rising sun and lifted my arms, as if I were drawing that ball of fire up from the earth and into the sky. There I was, encircled by rocks, at the center of the universe. And everything—from the dried-up riverbed to the limestone cliff outcroppings on the other side, even the glowing sky—watched me.

I closed my eyes as I stood in the circle, my back muscles relaxing, my arms stretched out, settling into their openness. I didn't know how long I stood there, but I listened to everything I could, to the mice rustling through the leaves, to the bending grasses, to the hollowness of the air over the cliff.

The sounds of home.

After a good, long while I stepped out of the ring of stones, my body lighter. I scanned the ground, as usual, looking for pebbles. I had to go a little farther from the circle, as I had found all the nearby pebbles a long time ago. I rummaged by the base of some grasses until I had five in my hand. Then I went over to a little crevice in the boulder, grabbed the thick, short stick I'd stashed there, and kneeled down in the area just outside the circle, in the upturned dirt where I'd buried the others.

I made five holes, wrapped my fingers around the first

pebble, and held it close to my mouth. "My birthday was horrible yesterday," I breathed into it, and my throat tightened as I spoke the words aloud. "It always is." Then I put the pebble in the hole and covered it up, patting the dirt lightly.

I took the second one, the pinkish one. "I want more," I whispered to it. I paused. It wasn't like a "I'm shopping and want to buy things" more, but something else. I couldn't figure out the words I wanted to say after that, so I just put the pebble in the ground.

I had buried quite a few pebbles for ponies. Well, ponies and scratch-n-sniff stickers and fireworks. That's what I'd first wanted when I started digging like this. Every time I put a pebble in the ground, something in me released, like the earth was holding my question or worry or secret and giving it an all-around hug. The earth could hold as many pebbles as I wanted to give it, and thinking about that felt so good that I buried pebbles every time I came. Couldn't stop if I tried.

I know people would call me crazy if they found out that I come to this cliff. I know that my parents would be angry and disappointed and afraid. But even though I've tried to stay away, this place calls me back as if it has a voice of its own.

Something is here.

Dad thinks the cliff is haunted by duppies. Maybe Bird's duppy is here instead of in heaven, where it belongs. But after coming here for four whole years, I think there are just some things no one is able to explain, not even Dad or Mom or mayors or priests. They think they know, but they don't.

I held the third stone in my hand. "There is this boy named John," I whispered. "I've never seen him around before—"

I paused. The hairs on my neck stood on end, in a wrongness kind of way.

Something awful was happening. Something really, really bad.

I didn't think about what it could be. I jumped to my feet and sped down the footpath, toward home.

I found Grandpa in the living room, slumped over on the floor, the TV blaring out some game show. Dad and Mom had gone by now, Mom to her part-time clerical job in Caledonia's town hall, Dad to sell gadgets at Max's Appliances three towns over, the only store like that for more than sixty miles.

"Grandpa!" I cried, shaking his body. He was cold. Unresponsive.

I felt my eyes grow wide. "No," I whispered.

I dashed through the house, looking for the case that held his diabetes emergency kit, which contained a vial of glucose that could save his life. I crashed into the bathroom and yanked open the medicine cabinet. It wasn't there. I ran into Grandpa's bedroom, even though I wasn't supposed to go inside, and rummaged through his nightstand, then his dresser drawers, then his closet. I was nearly ripping apart with fear: Even if I called Dad or Mom, it would take a half hour for them to drive home. An ambulance, too.

I spun around in a circle, my eyes searching furiously for the kit. Then I saw it: a small, clear box with a syringe and a vial inside. It was only the size of a pencil box, much smaller than what I had been looking for. In my panic, I had yanked it out of his nightstand and hadn't seen it fall to the ground.

I snatched the kit and ran back to the living room. I had seen Dad give Grandpa this shot only once, a long time ago, when he didn't think I was watching. Dad had injected the glucose in Grandpa's arm, deep into the muscle. I clenched my teeth, pulled the syringe out of the box, stuck it into the vial, and drew up the clear liquid. Then I plunged the needle into Grandpa's arm and injected the glucose into his body. Wild applause filled the room. I jumped and turned around. A participant on the game show had just tripled her money and won a trip to Bermuda. She was screaming and crying and waving her hands in the air.

I ran to the kitchen, picked up the phone, and dialed 911.

By the time the ambulance got to our house, Grandpa was already starting to move. I showed Mr. Williamson and Mr. Brendle, the town's two part-time paramedics, into the living room. They lifted Grandpa onto a wheeled bed and put him in the ambulance; his skin was a shock of color against the perfectly white sheet. I let my eyes linger on him, which felt weird since I never really let myself look at him. His body was lean but muscular, his chin firm, his cheekbones pointy and no-nonsense, and his short, wiry hair just lightly tipped with gray. I was amazed at how strong he looked, even in an ambulance. Maybe he thought he was strong enough to stop worrying about his blood sugar level, even though he should have known that if he let it drop that low it could kill him.

"Jewel?" Mr. Williamson was looking at me, tugging on the dark blue cuffs of his shirt.

I jumped. "Yes?"

"I said, how long was he unconscious?"

"I don't know. I wasn't home."

Mr. Williamson made a puzzled face. "You weren't?"

"No. I was at the cliff." The words came out just like that, like a tsunami was crashing out of my mouth.

Mr. Williamson straightened, and his face went hard. "The cliff?"

We both knew what cliff I was talking about.

I sealed up my lips, not revealing another secret. A tight silence surrounded us, and for what seemed a small eternity, I felt the weight of his questions and accusations and judgment.

I squirmed. "Is Grandpa going to be okay?"

Mr. Williamson looked at me and nodded, and he started talking about insulin and a lot of medical things I didn't understand. He talked more than he needed to, and the angle of the morning sun slowly blended away the stress lines on his face, his lines of apprehension at being at our house. He looked comfortable, almost.

But I knew better.

"Jewel," he said, pushing up his glasses on his nose, "are you going to come with us to the hospital? We'll need someone to translate . . ." He trailed off and his huge feet fidgeted on our gravel driveway. The entire town knew that Grandpa couldn't speak, or chose not to. There were even people at church who whispered he had a curse on his mouth for nicknaming my brother Bird.

I shook my head. "I called Dad, and he said he'll meet you there." Grandpa wouldn't want me that close to him in the ambulance, anyway. He also wouldn't say thank you to me for saving his life, of course. But truthfully, a grateful look would be nice.

Mr. Williamson nodded again and hopped into the ambulance, and the vehicle crunched on the gravel as they drove away. I walked back to the house, trying to take some deep breaths and calm my thumping heart. More than that, though, I tried to forget about the moment when Mr. Williamson's gaze faltered, when he looked at the house and at me with the strangest expression on his face, almost fearful, before he nodded his professional nod. I get that same look when I'm in town with Mom or Dad, from Mrs. Ballantine, who owns the hardware store, or from Mr. Stewart, the grocer. I wonder sometimes if people are afraid of us, of the circumstances of my birth, of Bird's death, of how we're mixing cultures and stories and magic that shouldn't be mixed. It did make my stomach flip, though, to get that same look from Mr. Williamson. Of course he would help us if we needed him.

At least, that's what I told myself.

CHAPTER THREE

IT TOOK a while to put back all the bottles and odds and ends in the bathroom. When I was done, I hesitated, wondering if I should go into Grandpa's room and try to put his things back too. I couldn't decide what was worse: him returning and finding his room an absolute mess, or finding that I'd gone through his things again and put them back incorrectly. In the end, I decided I should at least try to fix his room. It's not like he would yell at me.

Grandpa's room was just as it had been all my life. I'd been in there only once before, when I was four or five, looking for Foo Foo, my stuffed rabbit. Mom and Dad told me not to go in his room, but they didn't even have to say anything; it was more the frozen click of his door shutting each time he entered and exited that kept me away. I knew I shouldn't have been in there, but I had looked everywhere else and I was getting scared because I thought maybe I lost Foo Foo forever. There I was in his bedroom, calling for my rabbit, when Grandpa came into the room. I sensed more than saw him, and when I turned around, the air caught in my lungs.

It was the way he looked at me that terrified me, the dark features of his face pulling together into rage. I bolted out of there as fast as I could, ran into my room, and stayed there for the rest of the day. I told Mom I was sick, and when she brought me some canned soup, she happened to step on the tip of Foo Foo's ear, who was lying just beneath my bed.

Grandpa's room was exactly the same as it was then: empty, blue walls, a window with white blinds but no curtains, a dresser, a nightstand, and a bed, neatly made, with a dark green comforter. Nothing was on the bed, just like nothing was on top of his dresser or nightstand. Barren.

My eyes scanned the items on the floor. I had been a whirlwind, and Grandpa's things were scattered like debris across the room. Thin books about Louis Armstrong; yellowed receipts and scraps of paper with delicate, old penmanship; letters; packets of seeds with no names on them; a small, black-green-and-gold Jamaican flag. One by one I put these things back into his nightstand, as best as I could. There were faint smells coming from all his belongings too, and I found myself sniffing each item that I replaced and trying to name them: coconut oil, cinnamon, and the scent of falling rain.

I was putting Grandpa's shoes back in his closet when I saw an entire shelf of old cassette tapes tucked along his back closet wall. Mom had some cassettes of her favorite music and played them every once in a while, but she had maybe five of them, big and bulky and holding maybe only ten songs each. Here in Grandpa's closet, there had to be at least a hundred cassettes, maybe two hundred, and they were flawlessly stacked in their old, plastic cases. That was strange, since there was never music coming from Grandpa's room. No sound at all.

A box had fallen to the ground, not far from the shoes. A small picture box, one whose red cardboard lid had been opened and closed and held so many times the edges were a muted pink. I opened it up and saw a picture of Grandpa and a woman who had to be Granny. There was only one picture of her in our house, on the living room wall, and that was the only way I knew her—the only face and clothes, the only lighting. In these pictures, it was so strange seeing her with different clothes, a different angle and expression, but still with joy in the crinkles of her deep brown skin. Grandpa was in the picture this time, his arm casually around her waist. His arm was at her waist in all the other photos with her: the two of them in front of the car, at the park, at a waterfall, with my dad when he was younger and stood taller, somehow. And each time, there Grandpa was, looking square into the camera with a huge, endless, unstoppable smile on his face, a smile broad and dark like two diverging tectonic plates, a smile that says, *Come with me.* My heart pulled with thick throbbing, but I wouldn't let myself want that Grandpa too. I knew better than to want the impossible.

Then I came to the last five pictures. Grandpa and Bird on horseback, on the swings, in the forest. Bird blowing out candles. In the last one, Grandpa was holding Bird by the edge of the cliff, laughing. The trees were red and golden, and the sky a cold, showy blue. Bird had this huge grin on his face as he was trying to stick his fingers up Grandpa's nose. Grandpa's face was wide with joy and surprise.

Grandpa, who laughs and speaks and joys.

Bird, who lives.

Jewel, who doesn't.

Then I saw an old, yellowed piece of paper, folded up into quarters and lying at the bottom of the photo box. It was a drawing. With crayons. A boy was flying in the sky, with a line coming from him and in labored writing:

"Me." A man on the ground, smiling and waving: "Pooba."

Pooba. My mouth silently formed the word once, then twice. Bird had called Grandpa "Pooba."

I bit my bottom lip. Who were these people? Where was all this joy, and where does joy go when it leaves your family? Does it go to someone else's family, soak into the earth, or does it dissolve away like your breath in the winter? And if it doesn't leave like this, then why isn't there any left for me?

I placed the box back on the shelf and tried to arrange the rest of Grandpa's things. To my dismay, even though I tried to jam everything back in, it wouldn't fit—his nightstand had been so full that the drawer wouldn't close properly. I scribbled a note explaining what had happened and left it on his bed. I knew he wouldn't have asked me about it, but I felt I should tell him anyway.

The phone rang. It was Dad. He was already at the hospital, and Mom was there too. The doctors had stabilized Grandpa, but they would keep him all day and release him that night. Dad sounded tired, but there was something behind his voice. Something uncomfortable. I told him not to worry about me, and after we hung up I put on my shoes, feeling the need to get outside. My feet pulled me along, running down the road, and it wasn't long before I was headed back to McLaren's tree.

The third branch was empty. My lips puckered up a little, the same way my mom's do when she's disappointed. I climbed up to the third limb anyway. The first branch is always the hardest. In a year or so I'll be tall enough to get off the ground easier, but for now I had my rope tied and knotted around the first limb to help haul myself up. John must have used my rope too, I thought, as I climbed my way through the tree. I was surprised how proud that made me feel.

But it bothered me that I told Mr. Williamson about going to the cliff; I've been going to the cliff since I was eight, and I've never told a single soul. Today, however, that secret just plopped out. People here call Dad superstitious, and he wouldn't be happy knowing where I go. He would think Bird talks to me there, or Granny, or a duppy. Mom would be even more upset, but for different reasons. The very worst thing would be to not be able to go to the cliff, because then I wouldn't belong anywhere. So when it comes to things that matter, I've always been really good at being as quiet as a stick.

Except this morning with Mr. Williamson.

Up from my perch, I spotted John walking toward me through the humid cornfields. It wasn't too hard. He was like a spot of night roving through the sunshine. He waved at me, and I waved back. It felt a little strange to be waved to. Folks in Caledonia don't wave to each other; they mostly nod or smile, or the guys jerk their chins up slightly, like their necks have an itch. The nods and smiles I get in town are smaller than the ones everyone else gets—or maybe that's just my imagination. Regardless, John was waving like he meant it.

It was a little startling.

John's moon teeth glimmered again as he grinned up at me. "It's my tree, remember?" A hefty pair of binoculars hung around his neck.

I grinned back from my branch. "I don't know what you're talking about," I called.

He hauled himself up the tree—using my rope, just as I'd suspected—and before I knew it, he was sitting in a fork off the thick trunk, not too far from me. He was a good climber; most kids try to climb trees only with their arms, and anyone who knows anything about climbing knows that you have to use your legs, and you have to be smart about it. Like climbing rocks. You have to find the center of your power in your hips, shift your weight at exactly the right angle, at exactly the right time, and find the exact right next place to go to, or you'll get stuck.

John did not get stuck.

"How did you know I was here?" I asked.

He shrugged. "Binoculars."

"You were spying on me?" I didn't know whether to feel insulted or pleased.

"You can see a lot of things from my uncle's house if you have a good pair. I just happened to see you," he added. He raised the binoculars to his eyes and stared through a break in the leaves and into the sky. Puffy, white cumulus clouds gathered like glowing cotton candy, and endless white streams from planes crisscrossed overhead.

John was still looking at the planes. He adjusted the focus on his binoculars. "I bet those people never look down at us."

"Nope," I said, swinging my legs. The bark pressed into my skin. It used to hurt, but I got used to it a long time ago.

"I bet they never land anywhere close to here either."

"Nope."

"I bet they don't even wonder about us, like how we're wondering about them."

"There's nothing special about us, I guess."

John lowered his binoculars and looked at me appraisingly. Some birds hop-fluttered among the branches, chirping. He gestured to the patch of sky. "Those jet lines in the sky are called contrails, short for 'condensation trails.'"

I peered with him at the glowing white ribbons.

John put his binoculars back to his eyes. "The airplane's engine releases carbon dioxide and water vapor, and at that altitude, the water vapor condenses into water droplets or ice." He looked at me. "They're streams of artificial clouds."

I had never thought about contrails, and I told him so.

John's lips curled up at the edges, like he was happy he knew something I didn't.

But I know things too.

"The whole state of Iowa used to be covered with water," I said, tugging at some hair that had escaped from my ponytail.

"Really?" John smiled even more, like I was making it all up.

"The exposed bedrock of these parts is from the Paleozoic Era, in the Silurian Period, about four hundred million years ago," I said. "Iowa used to be a shallow inland sea and filled with brachiopods, trilobites, and stromatoporoids." I said that last word slowly. Stromatoporoids. It's one of my favorite words. "Over millions of years, their shells helped form rocks in this area—"

Then I noticed how he was staring at me bug-eyed. My face suddenly felt hot, and my lips fused shut. When I started learning about rocks, I told Dad about what I'd read in books and on the computers that they let you use in school. But he just shook his head and looked embarrassed, as if I were telling him something top secret—or worse, disappointing, like I'm not supposed to be turning out like this. "Don't tell your mom," he said to me. All the other girls were interested in their hair or the little makeup kits they got from Pickett, the largest town in the area, and not one of them ever talked about rocks or the earth or the secrets that came long before them. That's the thing with telling people what you know: You never know what they'll do with the information.

I had to change the subject. "Where are you from, anyway?"

His studied me. "How do you know all that?"

I swatted at a fat horsefly on my leg and shrugged, feeling smaller. It was suddenly stifling hot in the canopy of the tree.

"Tell me, or I'll throw these binoculars at you."

My head snapped up just in time for me to see a huge grin on John's face. I laughed, and it felt good. "You wouldn't dare."

"You're right. They're expensive binoculars."

I stuck my tongue out at him, and a spot between my shoulder blades relaxed. I paused. "I want to be a geologist when I grow up."

John nodded seriously. "You'd be a great one."

My heart tumbled out of my chest, off my branch, and onto the ground.

"Really," he continued. "You're not like the other girls in this stupid town, where they just want to be like each other. You climb trees at night. You do things by yourself."

I did things by myself because I didn't have a choice.

"Geologists need to set their own course." John nodded confidently. "All scientists do."

I stared at him. How was it I'd never heard about John before? Caledonia is so small that everyone doesn't just know everyone else's business, they actually know everyone else's business *before* that business becomes business. Like when the Rogers' house burned down in a lightning storm, we had a raffle and Belgian waffle fund-raiser, but the raffle tickets sold out even before they went on sale. That kind of thing. It was amazing that I'd never heard about Mr. McLaren's nephew John, because he sure is the kind of news that people like to talk about.

"Where are you from?" I asked John again.

"Not from here." He raised his binoculars again and studied the birds in the tree, but they were too close for the binoculars. Even I knew that.

"Why are you visiting your uncle?"

"Why does *anyone* visit their uncle? Because they have to."

I was surprised at how edged those words were, like scissors snipping through velvet. I was even more surprised at how he didn't want to visit his uncle. I would be excited to visit my uncles, any of them, if I knew them. The truth is, I don't even know if they exist, on either side.

"You're lucky," I said. "I'd visit my uncle, if I had one."

John's face went hard, like onyx. "Good for you."

The tension in the air suddenly grew so thick we didn't need tree limbs to sit on anymore, we could have sat on one of those words that just crawled out and got huge.

I shifted uncomfortably. It's not like I meant to make him mad or anything. I wanted to say something like, *Sorry for upsetting you*, like they do on TV shows, but I wasn't sure if people actually said things like that. Those words certainly aren't said in my family. They're just smothered by silence.

"Want to keep climbing?" I asked, scootching over to the trunk of the tree and standing up. "I can show you this squirrel's nest."

He looked at me, and his face shifted. Softened, no longer stone.

We climbed for hours that summer afternoon, sometimes talking, sometimes silent, sometimes sweating too hard to talk. Getting to know a tree is hard work. You have to know how its leaves smell in the heavy heat of summer, how its branches clatter against one another in the autumn winds, and how the rain pours in rivulets down its trunk and drips off its branches in the storms. It takes time, pure and simple. The same thing is true with getting to know the earth or a river or a person. By the time the shadows were long, we were both pretty tired and hungry. John headed back through the cornfields and I walked my slow way home, wondering about Grandpa and John and how so many things could happen in one day.

But something wasn't sitting right, and it chewed at the edges of my thoughts. As I turned up our mile-long driveway, it hit me: John hadn't come from the direction of Mr. McLaren's house, where he said he'd seen me. And when he left, he certainly wasn't headed back there.

CHAPTER FOUR

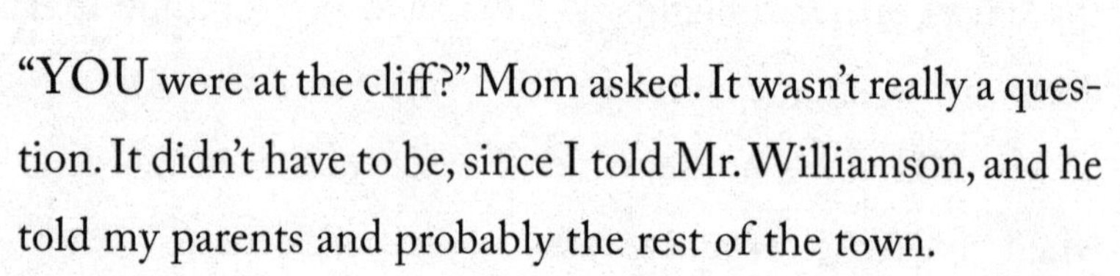

"YOU were at the cliff?" Mom asked. It wasn't really a question. It didn't have to be, since I told Mr. Williamson, and he told my parents and probably the rest of the town.

My feet fidgeted under the kitchen table. I couldn't look at her, or Dad, either. It didn't help that they had been waiting for me to get home for two whole hours—and that was *after* being delayed at the hospital. I had left a note, but I guess I forgot to tell them when I was going to come back. The only time they seem to remember me is when I'm in trouble. Which isn't that often, but still.

Mom glared at Dad. "You see what happens when she listens to your talk?" Her voice was low.

"Just this morning," I said. "Not this afternoon."

Dad shook his head, avoiding Mom's eyes. He stood in the doorway, away from both of us.

"You see what happens?" Mom said again. She punched the buttons on the microwave to reheat the rice and peas, plantains, and chicken that Dad made a couple days ago. She punched the buttons a lot harder than she needed to.

"Mr. Williamson said I found Grandpa just in time," I said, tucking my hands under my thighs.

"It wouldn't have been 'just in time' if you had been home," Mom said.

My stomach tightened. All the other kids would have been sleeping that early in the morning and all their grandpas would have died, I thought. I'd known that Grandpa wouldn't thank me, but I didn't expect this. Did no one notice that I'd saved his life this morning? Why was that difficult to see?

The microwave churned and hummed, warming our dinner. Dad finally moved from his doorway post and set the table, avoiding Mom as much as he could; when the microwave buzzer beeped, it cut through the heavy air, and we ate dinner with a cold clattering of metal on plates.

This is what I mean about silence. My parents didn't ask me why I went to the cliff, how often I go, or if they can go with me. They didn't ask how I feel when I go, or if I wonder about Bird, or if I wish I could fly after him. They didn't even tell me what it was like in the hospital, how scared they were, or how Grandpa was recovering. Or why he let his blood sugar drop so low in the first place.

It's almost as if we're afraid of words. They hang in the air, unspoken, and then seeing that they're not going to be used, they shrivel and die. It's no wonder that my mouth opened up this morning and made noise when it wasn't supposed to. Maybe my mouth is getting tired of keeping things pent up like that and spurted out a couple of words in protest. I can't blame it for going a little crazy with all the silence.

As we were finishing up, Dad wiped his lips with his napkin and looked at me. "Don't go back there, Jewel. It's not a good place."

"I know."

"There are duppies there, like I told you." He placed his hands on the table and rubbed his thumbnails, which meant he was worried. "The spirit world is not something to take lightly."

Mom sighed—almost inaudibly, but I heard it.

Dad pretended he didn't hear her. "I am very disappointed in you, Jewel."

I looked down at my plate. I'd known he would say that, but the words still gashed through me.

"You need to get a job," Mom cut in. "You have too much free time this summer."

And that was the end of the conversation. Dad went to check on Grandpa and give him his dinner, and I helped Mom clean up, but even though I scrubbed the table really good, just how she likes, she didn't look at me. Not once.

Mom was surprised at how hard it was for me to get a summer job. She kept saying she knew Mrs. Jameson needed help with her bakery deliveries, which I could do by bike, and the Matthews family had three kids that needed babysitting, and Mr. Perry's dog, Burger, always needed a walk. For some reason, though, no one seemed too interested when Mom brought up the idea of me helping out.

So instead, Mom made a list of things for me to do when she and Dad were at work.

Jewel's Summer Chores*:

1. Mondays: Pick up around the house
2. Tuesdays: Mow the lawn and weed the garden
3. Wednesdays: Vacuum
4. Wednesdays and Fridays: Visit Mrs. Rodriguez

5. Fridays: Clean the bathroom

*In general: Go through your closet, throw out your unwanted stuff from the attic, and kill the ants in the kitchen. (They keep coming back.)

The only chores that I didn't mind were mowing the lawn, because the riding lawn mower was pretty fun, and weeding Dad's garden. Dad grows all kinds of flowers and vegetables, and even plants from Jamaica, but they never amount to anything more than a couple of droopy sprouts, as if the Iowan soil only wants to see corn and tomatoes pop up, not coconut and soursop and breadfruit trees. He often lets me help him garden, because he knows how much I love to dig in the earth. I do it when I'm upset—I just go and find some earth, and I dig. It may sound strange, but there's something about making your arms work harder than they want to, about turning your hands into claws and your shoulders into motors and digging until you find things that you never saw before, things that you wouldn't have seen unless you dug.

Like arrowheads.

Mom doesn't like it when I find arrowheads. She tells me to stop wasting my time, stop daydreaming, and how can I be a teacher when I waste my brain digging in the dirt like a dog?

"But I don't want to be a teacher," I told her once when we were folding clothes. "I want to be a geologist." Mom looked at me when I said that, looked good and hard, to see if I was lying. Of course, I wasn't.

"I want you to have a nice, practical job," she said.

"Geologists are practical," I told her. "They're scientists."

"Digging in the backyard is not science," Mom replied curtly as she held Dad's T-shirt in her hands. "It's daydreaming, just like your dad." She looked up to the ceiling, like she couldn't believe she was having this conversation. Then she started folding clothes again, pressing each fold carefully, like I had never said anything at all.

I never mentioned being a geologist again.

But being a geologist was the only thing I could think about as I weeded Dad's garden. How fantastic is it that Iowa used to be the bottom of a shallow sea, like the Gulf of Mexico, and that our hills, rolling and swelling like the ocean, used to be actual waves? The dirt that my hands scoop up used to be brachiopods, echinoderms, and corals. They used to be living and swimming, and now they're dirt. And everything that's living now will someday be dirt too.

Dirt is everything.

I'm not sure how weeding will help me become a teacher.

"Need any help?"

I jumped and twisted my head up toward John's voice. His jean shorts and T-shirt looked incredibly clean next to my grubby, dirt-covered clothes. "How'd you know I live here?" I said. I was more alarmed that I'd get in trouble for having someone over than the fact that, again, John had found me. Mom would say a guest would distract me from my chores.

John tried to hide a smile. "Looks like there's a lot of weeds to be pulled."

I sighed. "I'm learning how to be a teacher."

John's eyebrows raised briefly. He knelt down next to me and started pulling up weeds and tossing them into my pile. "Not a geologist? They pick rocks, not weeds."

"They pick weeds when their mothers tell them to," I said, ripping out a fistful of deep dandelion roots. Sweat already prickled my forehead. "Don't say too much about geology around here," I said. "Mom doesn't like it."

We worked side by side under the lifting June sun, weeding our way through Dad's garden. It was nice to have someone help me.

"What are these plants?" John asked, pointing at Dad's tiny sprouts of coconut and soursop and breadfruit.

"They're Jamaican tree saplings," I said. "Dad thinks they'll grow here. He wants a grove."

John gave me a look. "In Iowa?"

"I know. Wrong soil."

"Wrong everything." John grunted as he dug up some thick roots.

I yanked another weed. "But he keeps telling me that maybe they'll get used to it."

John paused. "That tropical trees will get used to Iowa?" he asked slowly.

I nodded. I knew how stupid it sounded. Dad can be kind of optimistic like that.

"Huh." John sat back on his heels and looked at the contrails in the sky. "Your dad's something else, you know." He studied the planes overhead.

"The cerasee is doing better than the trees," I said, pointing to one corner of the garden. "I keep telling him to give up on the saplings, but he says those trees are good for the duppies."

That got his attention. "The what?"

"Duppies," I said. John was looking at me strangely, so I continued. "You have a soul and a spirit, and when you die, the soul goes to heaven and the spirit stays on earth for a couple more days with the body. If someone's tears fall on the body during the funeral, or if something else like that happens, then the spirit is stuck on earth and haunts people. Makes trouble."

John's eyes were pretty big by now.

"Duppies don't like some kinds of trees and plants," I continued, "and if you plant them around your house, it helps keep them away."

"Really."

"It's a Jamaican thing."

We weeded for a while in silence, and then he said, "What kind of trouble do duppies make?"

"I don't know," I said, even though every fiber in me was screaming, *Bird*. I lowered my face between my shoulders so he couldn't see my lie.

"Do you believe in that stuff?" John asked.

I couldn't look at him even if I wanted to. "I don't think so," I said slowly. I'm not sure if I believe in duppies and souls and spirits, but a part of me felt like I was disrespecting Dad right then, because he does.

We do all believe that Grandpa killed my brother when he gave him the nickname Bird. Names are important, and even though Grandpa didn't mean to, he attracted a duppy into the house who followed my brother and convinced him to jump. Mom doesn't believe in duppies, being a Catholic—

not that we go to church much. She thinks that Grandpa killed Bird because his talk messed up Bird's mind, got him confused. He was only a little kid, after all. "Loose lips sink ships," she spat at Dad once, when they were arguing about Grandpa, "but loose lips killed our son."

"Duppies." John was shaking his head. "That's crazy." He glanced at me. "No offense."

There. He said it. *That's crazy.* I gave a little shrug, like I didn't care very much about what he thought, but my lips sure zipped up tight. I was glad I didn't mention anything about the cliff like I did with Mr. Williamson, and I decided right then not to say anything else important, like ask where John was headed to yesterday. Or where he really *really* came from.

Instead, I said, "So where will you go when you're an astronaut? Mars?"

John tossed a couple more weeds into a new pile. "Nah. Mars is overrated. I'll go to Jupiter's moons."

"Moons? More than one?" A trickle of sweat ran down my neck. A rock crushed into my knee, and my back was starting to get tight on me. Weeding was more work than I remembered.

"Jupiter has over sixty moons." John sat back on his haunches. "The biggest ones are Io, Europa, Ganymede, and

Callisto. I'm going to be the first astronaut to land on those."

Sixty moons. Imagine how great Jupiter's night sky would be.

Just then I heard something behind me, and I turned.

Grandpa.

Grandpa, who never comes near me. The air grew colder, like he was freezing everything around him, including every limb in my body. He stood not ten feet away from John and me, on the grass, in his boxers and a thin, white T-shirt.

I sucked in my breath and struggled to my feet, averting my gaze. "Grandpa, this is John."

"Hey there," John said, standing up and wiping his hands on his shorts. He extended his hand to Grandpa.

Grandpa's eyes were as big as eggs.

John's hand was still stuck out, warm and friendly.

Grandpa was still staring. I never saw him stare before; usually he makes it a point not to look at anything.

"We met yesterday," I said, trying to shake the ice from under my skin.

Suddenly, Grandpa's nostrils flared, and his eyes squinted into slits.

John put his hand down.

The sun stopped climbing up the sky.

Then, to my horror, Grandpa smacked his lips and spit on the ground, by John's feet, and he made an X in the grass with his toe.

John backed up a couple inches and his jaw dropped. If I were him, I would have just run away. But John's back straightened and he lifted his chin slightly. "I'm sorry if I did something wrong," he said, "but the garden is weeded. I hope you have a nice d—"

Grandpa scowled and made a funny gesture with his hand, one that I'd never seen before. Then he made another X in the ground.

John's mouth fell open. It was as if his words had dropped, midair, from shock.

I hung my head and waited to hear John's footsteps as he walked away. I waited to hear him say that with all the craziness that's in my family, I didn't deserve his company. A lump formed in my throat. John had seemed like he really wanted to be my friend.

I had been so close.

"Come on," John said to me. "Let's go somewhere."

I yanked my head up. Grandpa had moved back about ten feet away from us, listening to every word. John was talking as if Grandpa wasn't even there.

"Come on," John insisted, grabbing my arm.

"B-but I haven't done my chores yet," I stuttered. "Mom will be mad."

John's brow furrowed. "But she wouldn't be mad that he"—John jerked his head at Grandpa—"just spat at me? Come on. It'll only be for a little while."

I bit my lip. I don't disobey my parents. Not intentionally. I know a lot of kids in my class don't listen to their parents, or they sneak out, or they talk all disrespectfully. But it's different for me. It's like, my parents have already lost Bird. I'm Bird's replacement.

At least, that's how it feels sometimes.

"Come on," John said again, exasperated. "I want to show you something."

Grandpa frowned.

I shuddered and leaned away from Grandpa, and in that moment I had a crushing desire to go with John, wherever he wanted to take me. Someplace other than my silent and cold house. I took a couple hesitant steps toward John.

Suddenly, Grandpa dashed at me and gripped my upper arm, his fingers like a vise.

"Let me go!" I cried, and I jerked my arm back violently. Then, before I knew what was happening, John started running and I was running after him, away from my house, my chores, my grandpa, and through the rows of growing corn.

CHAPTER FIVE

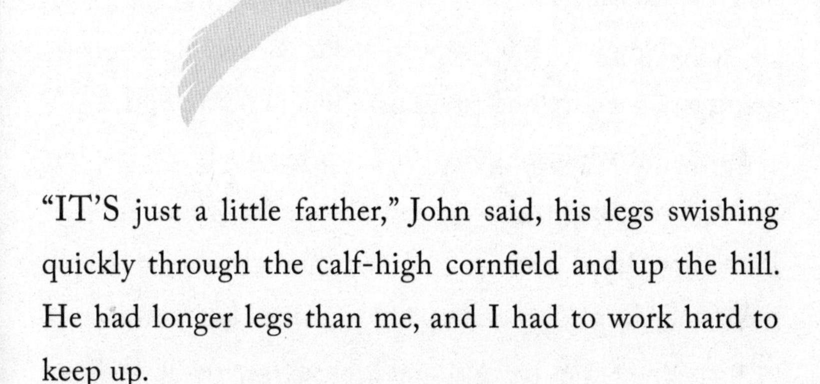

"IT'S just a little farther," John said, his legs swishing quickly through the calf-high cornfield and up the hill. He had longer legs than me, and I had to work hard to keep up.

I felt tingly and strange all over, like my body didn't belong to me. Did I really just do that? Did I disobey my grandpa, right to his face? My stomach churned with shame. Would he tell my parents? That would be even worse.

My foot caught on a dip in the earth, and I fell to my knees. John stopped and came back. "You okay?" he asked.

"It's nothing," I said, even though a little rock had hit my kneecap hard.

"Just wait until you see this place I want to show you,"

John said, and his smile was so bright I wondered for the two hundredth time why Grandpa was so angry at him. John helped me to my feet. "What was up with your grandpa? He went nuts back there."

"I don't know," I said, and that was the true-blue truth. "Maybe he was in a bad mood." That wasn't quite true, but it was better than saying that Grandpa didn't like John for no good reason.

"A bad mood," John repeated. He looked like he was going to say something else, then thought better of it.

I thought we were going to go to his uncle's house but instead we went in the opposite direction, where I'd seen John come from yesterday. We cut through three different fields and climbed up a steep hill to a small but dense grove of trees that sat at its crest and looked over the land. Iowa isn't all cornfields, unlike what a lot of people think; it has a lot of variety to it, with bluffs and caves and sinkholes and oxbow lakes. And it's not flat, either; its hills swell and dip, a river of land flowing from the Rockies in the west, rolling like waves on the horizon.

The sun was high overhead now, and my throat itched with thirst. Iowa is no place to mess around without water in the summer. With it being a landlocked state and all, the heat just swelters and bakes everything it touches. All the folks with air conditioners hide in their houses. My family has to sweat it out.

We slowed down when we reached the thin, outlying trees, which seemed to sweat in the summer heat. The trees farther in got bigger, thicker; with their protective canopy they became a grove of mothers holding out their arms, shielding us from the sun. Leaves bent softly beneath our feet, and John guided me through the glowing understory, until he suddenly stopped.

"Here."

I looked up. In front of me stood an enormous hollow tree, a basswood, much taller and larger than all the rest. It pierced through the canopy with its bare branches and naked trunk. It was dead, for sure; it must have died long ago from lightning or fungus or old age. The heartwood was completely gone, dissolved away, almost, but the bark and shell of the trunk and all its branches stood firmly intact. A four-foot-high hole rose from its base, like a door.

It was a house. Made of a tree.

"What happened to it?" I said. I was almost whispering.

"I don't know," John said, and he seemed a little embarrassed. "I was hoping you would."

I shook my head.

"This is Event Horizon," John announced. His chest puffed out a little.

"What?"

"The name of my tree," he said.

I found myself grinning again. "It's not your tree, you know."

John's dark eyes twinkled. "Trees belong to everyone. Check it out."

The temperature seemed to drop twenty degrees inside the tree, and the ground was soft, spongy beneath my feet. As my eyes adjusted to the shadows, I could make out the dark, rich walls of wood encircling me, and I squinted up at the bright disk of sky overhead. It smelled of peat moss and loam, the scent of one thing slowly becoming another. It's funny, I realized, that people feel like they have to go into churches to pray when there is all this sacredness sitting here, outside, silent and waiting.

"It's really great to come here at night," John said. I hadn't even heard him enter, the ground was so soft. "You see the stars when you look up."

"Like a spaceship," I said, and the moment I said it, I knew I was right. I turned around slowly, my neck craned up, taking it in.

He nodded and handed me a bottle of water. I looked at him, grateful but confused.

"Over by the doorway," John said.

I had missed it when I ducked inside: a little stash of water, candy bars, flashlights.

"Awesome," I whispered.

No one had ever shown me their secrets. In my family we hoard our secrets, gathering them in with greedy arms, never sharing them with anyone. And now that John had shown me his secret place, it was like the universe was unrolling before me.

I felt rich.

Then it hit me. "This is where you were coming from yesterday."

He pressed his lips together. "It's better than home."

Anyone could see why being at Event Horizon was way better than being at some dumb house with nothing to do.

"So does your grandpa spit at every person he meets?" John asked.

I winced. I'd nearly forgotten about it. "No, he's just . . ." I searched for the word. "Different."

"Really."

"No, I mean, besides that. He doesn't talk."

"Not at all?" John ducked out of Event Horizon, and I followed after him. We sat down some ten feet from the tree, drinking our water and watching the sun cast mottled patches of light on our legs.

"He hasn't talked since my brother died."

A pause. "I'm sorry."

I squirmed. I hate it when people say *I'm sorry* when I mention my brother. "It's okay," I said, "I never knew him." And, I realized, I never really knew Grandpa, either.

An awkward silence fell over us, and my hands started digging into the cool soil.

John watched me dig for a moment, then looked back at his tree. "Event Horizon's a great tree, but I don't climb it."

Dead trees are dangerously brittle. I let the dirt sift through my fingers. "Why do you call it Event Horizon?" I asked.

John gave a little knowing nod, as if he'd expected me to ask that. "You've heard of black holes, right?"

"Right." I hesitated. "A little bit."

"When a supergiant star dies, it implodes—crashes in on itself—and forms a black hole. Everything gets sucked into it. Even light. Stars too."

"Where does all that stuff go?"

John shrugged. "No one knows. Anyway, if people were able to get into a black hole, there'd be no way to tell us what was on the other side, because they couldn't get out."

He had a point.

"The black hole's pull is strong, but you can avoid getting sucked in if you don't get too close. The event horizon is what scientists call that point of no return. You cross it . . ." John pointed a finger and crossed his neck with it. "Ack. You're sucked in. Good-bye. If you don't cross the event horizon, you can still get free."

I thought it sounded scary to name a favorite tree as the point of no return. But it sounded daring, too. I would have never thought of a name like that.

"If you ever get sucked into a black hole, where do you think you'll end up?" I asked.

"Another dimension," John replied simply.

How could he be so confident? My head buzzed a little. I'd never met anyone like him before. And the best thing was that someone as confident and courageous and smart as John was happy sitting in the woods with me. In my whole life, I hadn't met someone who truly understood why I dig in the dirt so much, or why I like rocks and trees or watch how the sky moves during a storm. But John liked all those things too, and then some, and he didn't feel he had to hide anything at all. I wanted to slip under his skin and snatch some of that confidence. Maybe that's why I told John that the other oaks and pine trees surrounding us looked really great for climbing.

John shot me a mischievous grin. "These trees go up a lot higher than my uncle's."

My lips twisted up. "Are you saying I'm afraid?"

"I'm saying that you can see everything."

We spent a long time climbing as high as we dared, and trying all kinds of different trees. He was right; there were some big trees with pretty daring jumps, from one branch to another to another, and at times I got a little nervous, but I kept up, right there with him.

We secured ourselves in the forking branches of a maple tree, and John was on the higher branch when he looked down at me. "What was your brother's name?"

I paused. I wasn't quite sure what to say, but then I realized I'd already lied to him about not believing in duppies and wasn't ready to tell two lies in one day, so I said, "John."

He swiped the sweat off his forehead and fixed his eyes on me. "No way."

My heart was thumping a little faster, and my hands gripped the bark until my fingers hurt. I wasn't quite sure what he was thinking. "Serious. But they called him Bird."

"Why?"

"Grandpa wanted him to fly."

We didn't say much after that, just kept climbing. There were still a couple big branches left before it got dicey, but we didn't go any higher. When our forearms ached too much, we climbed down, ate John's snacks, and stood at the edge of the grove. From the top of the hill, we could see the flowing, green-golden land, the tiny little houses below—with a clear view of my house and Mr. McLaren's, too—carved dolomite cliff formations, and the gravel roads as thin as twigs in the distance. Millions upon millions of years of earth were holding us.

When I snuck a peek at John, I caught him looking to the sky.

Dad was standing by his garden when I got home, hands on his hips, studying each plant.

"Hey, Dad," I said, giving him a light peck on the cheek, but my stomach twisted inside. If Grandpa had somehow told him how I'd disobeyed him this afternoon, I would be in deep trouble. "What do you think of the weeding?" I asked as casually as possible.

He was nodding his head. "Nice job, Jewel," he said. Dad bent down and inspected the young cucumber leaves.

I exhaled silently, relieved. Grandpa hadn't said anything.

"I'm surprised you got all the way down beneath those prickers," Dad continued. "Their roots are tough."

Those were the weeds that John pulled up.

Dad walked slowly around the perimeter. "I was starting to worry about the rosemary."

My cheeks felt hot. I wasn't sure I had done something wrong. "It looks pretty healthy to me," I said.

He put his hand on my shoulder. "Yes, but if those weeds had strangled out the rosemary, that would be very bad for us."

"It would be unlucky because rosemary protects us," I said, more confidently this time.

Dad's eyebrows lifted with delighted surprise. "You remembered."

I beamed. Dad had told me about rosemary a long time ago, and I had run to my room to write down what he'd said so I could impress him at a time exactly like this. "Rosemary can be used in different ways," I said. I scrunched my brow, thinking. "You rub it on your skin or put it in your pocket when you need help remembering things. Like for tests."

"And?"

"And . . . you put it under your pillow so you don't get nightmares."

He squeezed my shoulder.

"And drinking rosemary tea can make you healthy if you get hurt," I added, wanting to make him even prouder.

"And?"

"And . . ." I faltered. I couldn't remember anything else.

"You burn rosemary to get rid of duppies," Dad said. "Burning rosemary is very powerful for warding them off."

"Just like the Xolo dog?" I asked.

Dad's smile grew wider. "Do I have a smart girl or what?" he said, shaking his head, but I knew it wasn't really a question.

Dad had been really excited when some show on TV talked about the Xolo dog, an ancient dog that protected the Aztec kings from intruders and evil spirits. After Dad found that out, he made sure a Xolo dog figurine was in our house. When I pointed out that Xolo dogs are from Mexico, not Jamaica, he replied that protective spirits do the same job, no matter where they're from. Then he made sure to work on the leak over in Mrs. Rodriguez's kitchen, because she was the one who brought the figurine back from Mexico for him. Dad put the little dog right by our family pictures in the living room, and it stayed there even though Mom had some sharp words for him when she got home.

There are a lot of things that Dad does that Mom's not too thrilled about. Especially taking care of our Buick. Even though it's super old, Dad makes sure to wash and wax it every Saturday afternoon, and he even has this special cloth mitt to put the wax cream on and a different mitt to take it off. Mom says all that is a waste of money, especially the car magazines that he leaves around the house. In her opinion, what would really help is if he could figure out how to fix the car when it breaks down, but I doubt Dad would notice even if the engine was missing, because never in my life have I seen him open up the hood. He sure shines the top of it, though, and when he's done waxing the Buick, he puts his hands on his hips, gives a little whistle, and nods his head. But we still have to take it in for everything, even an oil change.

I guess I don't blame him for being as proud as a peacock about that Buick, even though it has rust on the sides. When he talks about the day he got that car, his whole face becomes as bright as a star, and his eyes twinkle too; he purchased it with cash, a big, rolled wad of it, and drove away in his spanking-new car, with a hot wife to boot. That's how he put it. I can just see the two of them smiling from ear to ear, their happiness gleaming like sunlight off the chrome. And even though he doesn't tell that story much anymore, I wonder sometimes if he still remembers it, especially because he's always waxing that car alone.

Dad and I stood at the edge of the garden in silence for a while, looking at how everything was growing. "The tree saplings don't look too good," I admitted.

Dad's eyes squinted up, like he was trying to make the

trees grow by sheer willpower. "Don't worry, honey. These are lucky saplings." His voice was a soft, gentle baritone. "I want them because they're good for protection too."

I scratched my arm. "Dad?" I asked.

"Yes?"

"If the rosemary is good for protecting us from duppies, why are you trying to grow the trees?"

Dad smiled. "You sure are one smart girl," he said, and put his arm around me. I leaned into him a little more. "The more protection around you, the better," he said. "It's like layers."

"Layers?" I cocked my head up at him.

"Layers of protection, Jewel. And you always want them nice and thick." He was nodding at the garden. "One day these will grow to be huge trees, you'll see."

I gave him a sideways look. "Coconut trees in a snowstorm?"

He chuckled. "Why not?"

I elbowed him.

"Hopefully they'll get to the point where we can transplant them into pots and bring them in the house for the winter. Then we'll wheel them in and out when they get bigger."

Like I said, Dad can be somewhat of an optimist. What happens when the coconut tree is taller than our house? But he doesn't bother with details like that. One reason why I think Dad loves these plants so much is that this used to be

Granny's garden, and Granny used to love plants too. Dad says she had a big garden in Jamaica in the countryside, and she knew the healing properties for all kinds of plants—plenty more than Dad knows about, from what he tells me. Maybe Dad feels closer to Granny by working the garden, like her spirit is still around, somehow. A lot of plants died when she did—Dad didn't know how to take care of them, but he told me they died because they were heartbroken—and the ones that lived he's super careful with. Granny knew a whole lot about duppies, too—like how to know when one's around—and Dad tries to teach me about them when Mom's not listening. Sometimes I think he wants to be more like Granny, because he'd talk about her and plants and duppies all day long if Mom would let him, but he doesn't. Instead, he looks at Granny's picture in our living room when he thinks I'm not watching; he just stands there and stares at Granny, like she's going to jump out of the picture frame and talk to him. She died when I was young, and it's strange that Dad misses so much someone I never really knew.

Dad and I inspected the garden for a long time, poking the plants here and there, rubbing their leaves, and smelling their fragrances. What made me the happiest, though, was that he didn't have to say not to mention any of our talk about rosemary to Mom. He knew I already knew that.

It's funny that it's Dad who's taking care of Jamaican plants, talking about duppies and the like, because he didn't come over from Jamaica—Grandpa and Granny did. Nobody's been back there either. Nothing to go back to, Dad said when I asked him once. Everything's changed by now—the people and towns are all different. Anyway, he said, he and Grandpa have been in the North so long that even the Jamaican sun wouldn't recognize them anymore. They'd probably get sunburned like a bunch of white people. Dad had laughed pretty hard when he said that. Still, once I found a really old travel flyer for a vacation package to Jamaica that was tucked into one of his car magazines. The flyer had these pictures of the ocean, and trees and sunsets, and the package included airfare and hotel and even meals, and listed what it said was a rock-bottom price. But that price didn't look very low to me. Maybe not to Dad, either, because he never said a word about it to us.

Dad's never even gone back to Miami, either. That's where Grandpa and Granny lived after they came over and where he grew up. I figured they'd want to go back and visit their friends, at least a couple times.

Sometimes I feel bad for Dad because he can't talk to

folks around here about things like using rosemary to ward off duppies. Iowa doesn't have the greatest Jamaican community, if you know what I mean. We have to drive fifty minutes to get to a store that sells plantains, and since those are sold for the Mexican Americans, that's the only time that Mom speaks Spanish, because the workers don't speak much English. Then we have to drive more than three hours to get to Chicago, where we buy our Jamaican food: saltfish, tinned ackees, Scotch bonnet peppers, dried pimento, bammies, and beef patties. After eating at our favorite Jamaican restaurant, we drive back to the cornfields, to the community that thinks that Jamaica is some country in Africa, to a place where the white people and the Latinos stay in their own little corners of town, and where mixing just doesn't happen.

Except for in my family.

I wonder what it would be like, sometimes, to have two parents who have the same languages and histories and recipes. It would make things less interesting, I think, but maybe a little simpler, too. When we leave Caledonia to go shopping, it's confusing to hear folks ask me what I am. Shouldn't they ask *who* I am? Why am I a *what*? I'm not sure why it matters so much, but I can tell by the way they stare that it does.

"Why didn't you pick up around the house?" Mom asked me, more tired than stern. It must have been stressful for her at work today or she would have been more upset with me. She had turned on the oscillating fan and was taking off the earrings Dad had given her for Christmas a couple years ago. Mom then leaned in to the mirror, staring at her face. She always looks for wrinkles or something on her smoky quartz skin. She doesn't know how much I'd love to look like her one day; she's so beautiful.

I was sitting on the edge of their bed, and I stopped swinging my feet back and forth. One day they'll touch the ground, but for now, they were still a couple inches away. "I didn't get to the living room because I got distracted a little." Heat rose to my face.

Mom's dark eyebrows rose and scrunched together. "By what?"

"I spent too much time weeding the garden." That was true, but not completely. I just left out the part about Grandpa, and then John, and then Event Horizon.

Mom sighed, and she turned to face me. "Jewel, come here."

I slipped off the bed and approached her, slowly. She gave me a hug, not too tight, then drew me back a ways so she could look at me. "I'm really worried about you, honey," she said.

I swallowed.

"You listen too much to your dad. He means well, but I want you to have a good job when you grow up. Be someone."

I squirmed. She was afraid that I won't? That I'm not anyone right now? I looked back at her and nodded.

"Your father is a sweet man, and you know I love him, but you can't take him too seriously."

I didn't like this conversation. I love Dad's lessons and his stories and the way he keeps wishing for things, even if they'll never come true. So what if he wants a coconut tree in Iowa?

Mom softly pinched my chin. "You're all we got, Jewel. I want you to make us proud."

A small tremor ran through me, like my heart was splitting, a deep crack in the earth, and all kinds of dark fears rose up. I swallowed.

"I want to make you proud too." I whispered. And nothing could have been truer than that.

Although Mom didn't say it, I could tell she was sad, just like I could tell all the other times when something inside her would wither away. Sometimes it would happen around my birthday, the anniversary of Bird's death, and she would change. Then she'd do a lot of the same things, but there'd be a deep heaviness in her eyes, and she would be quiet a lot, and sometimes she'd cry, like at the dinner table for no reason, and when she would speak all she could do was tell me I did something wrong. She'd get mad a lot too, more than normal. That was the worst part, when she'd get mad, because there'd be nothing I could do to make things better.

Every time she changed like this, it was about Bird. Sometimes I'd be scared about my birthday because I'd be afraid that Mom would turn sad or angry—and she wouldn't be like this just for a day but for weeks or months sometimes, until something would happen and snap her out of it. The tricky thing was that you never knew when it would come; sometimes my birthday would pass and Mom would stay Mom, laughing more than I thought possible on my birthday.

I'd always know when Mom had returned because she'd rub me on the back in the old way. But Mom would change every once in a while—sometimes around my birthday, sometimes when I would ask about Bird, like that time I asked what his favorite food was. When this would happen, I'd get so mad at myself for bringing Bird up at all. So, of course, I learned not to bring him up. It was just too risky. But even though I'd learned to stay far away from talking about Bird, she'd still slip into this other Mom, and then I'd wonder what I did to make her do that. Like, she turned sad a couple weeks before my twelfth birthday, and I got really mad at myself for having a birthday in the first place.

Grandpa emerged from his room for dinner, sat down at his chair, and stared at his empty plate. He sucked on his cheeks. I bit my lip and continued to set the table, trying not to think about how I'd left with John, defying him.

"How are you feeling?" Dad asked Grandpa. Dad was asking this a lot since they got home from the hospital yesterday.

Grandpa shrugged dismissively. Then he angled his head just slightly in my direction and frowned good and angry and deep.

I pretended not to notice and brought over the tortillas and rice and beans, some zucchini that Mom managed to fry up, and Mrs. Rodriguez's salsa. It was Mom's dinner night. It's funny, because Dad learned to cook Mexican food from Mrs. Rodriguez and cooks it a whole lot better than Mom does. Mom doesn't like to cook so we get a lot of canned beans, even though they're more expensive than the dried ones. And she loves salsa, but Dad doesn't make it well, so they send me to Mrs. Rodriguez's house to get some. Mrs. Rodriguez doesn't speak any English, and she always gives me these looks when I drop by, like she pities me. I'm not sure if she pities me because Mom didn't teach me Spanish or because I'm kind of skinny and Mom's not a good cook, but whatever. I get our salsa from her in exchange for Dad shoveling for her in the winter.

We'd just started dinner when I noticed that Grandpa wasn't eating. That was strange, since he usually digs in and doesn't stop until he cleans his plate. Mom glanced at Dad.

"Grandpa? What's wrong?" Dad asked.

My stomach flip-flopped. He was going to tell them what I did. I felt like throwing up.

Suddenly, Grandpa grabbed his knife and fork, and with both fists started pounding his silverware on his plate. I gasped and jumped back from the table.

The three of us stared at one another as Grandpa's metallic pounding filled the room.

"Grandpa," Dad said, getting up, but Grandpa was already stalking into the kitchen. Mom looked at me, wide-eyed. We ran over in time to see Grandpa carrying our ten-gallon rice container to the screen door. Dad and Grandpa wrestled over it until, with the shoving and pulling, they spilled it all over the kitchen floor. The hard grains skittered over the linoleum in a white, dry waterfall. Grandpa opened the door and started kicking the rice out of the house, onto the ground.

Dad pinned Grandpa's arms behind his back. "Grandpa! Stop this! There are no duppies here!"

My stomach dropped, and blackness crept around my vision. I grabbed the counter to steady myself. Dad and Mom struggled with Grandpa, step by crunching step, slipping on the rice, to get him out of the house. Dad's engine started, and then he and Grandpa were gone.

I blinked away the blackness. Mom staggered back into the house, letting the door slam behind her. In that instant, the look she gave me was one of pure bewilderment and fear. The next moment, though, her face returned to its usual controlled state, like a curtain going down over her, until she was gone too.

Silently we got down on all fours and began to gather the rice that Grandpa had spilled, the rice that somehow was supposed to keep the duppy away, the rice that we were going to eat the next day, and the next day, and the next.

"Wasn't Mrs. Rodriguez's salsa good?" Mom said calmly.

I nodded. Yes, it was.

CHAPTER SIX

"HOW old is the earth?" John asked a few nights later, when I had slipped away to Event Horizon to meet up with him.

"About four and half billion years," I said. We were inside the tree and had just finished saving the Andromeda Galaxy from aliens and quasar explosions and giant black holes. Mom and Dad go to bed pretty early, so they didn't notice I had slipped out. I leaned my back against the inside of the trunk and chewed on one of John's granola bars.

"Four and a half billion? Is that all?"

I shined my flashlight on his face.

"Hey!" he said, turning his face away from the light beam.

I hid a smile. "What do you mean, 'Is that all'? That's a long time."

"Not compared to the age of the universe."

"Four and a half billion years is still a long time."

John snorted.

"If four and a half billion years amounted to the span of one calendar year, then humans have been on earth for the equivalent of twenty-three minutes." That was my favorite factoid in all the world, taken right from my favorite geology book.

John paused. "Twenty-three minutes?"

"Yup." I stuffed the rest of the granola bar into my mouth. "Dinosaurs roamed the earth about two weeks ago." That was my second favorite fact.

"But what happened in the time before that?"

I shrugged. "Precambrian. Most of January through November."

John made figure eights on the tree wall with his flashlight. "Well, light travels at the speed of 186,000 miles per second, and in a year it covers almost 5.9 trillion miles," he said. "That's a light-year. The closest star to us besides the sun is Proxima Centauri, which is about four light-years away."

That was about 24 trillion miles. My head hurt thinking about a trillion anything.

"And since the light from that star has taken four years to reach us," John said, "it could have exploded by now and we wouldn't know about it for years!" He hit the dirt with his fist.

"Why do you want to be an astronaut?" I said.

John tilted his head back to look at the stars through the hole in the roof of the tree. "I want to find what's out there," he said. He was quiet for a moment. The cicadas were almost deafening. "This planet is just a tiny speck compared to the universe."

I crumpled my granola wrapper into my pocket. "Won't you be lonely?"

"I could go anywhere. Like Ganymede. Io. Beyond."

"But won't—"

"I don't need anyone."

I didn't know what to say. John sounded a little silly right then, since he has to need someone, like his parents or his uncle, for food and stuff. But his words were angry, just how Grandpa's silence was angry, or how anger hid beneath the surface of Mom and Dad's words or the way they brushed their teeth or the way they hugged each other, even. And when anger peeks above the surface, it's like rice, spilling over everywhere, and no matter how hard you try to clean it up, it sticks in the corners, impossible to get out.

After Dad came back with Grandpa—they had gone out for a ride, to cool off—Grandpa stayed in his room for two days straight, leaving only to go to the bathroom. But his presence was colder than ever, a cold that went much deeper than our howling winters, a cold that came from someplace awful within. And even worse, Dad didn't go out to check on his garden that entire time. He's always out there after work, poking around, inspecting the growing leaves. But ever since Grandpa spilled the rice, not once did Dad tend to his garden. I watered his saplings for him.

I was thinking of Grandpa and Dad and the rice and the silences and I didn't think my mouth was planning on doing anything about it, but I was wrong because the words came out: "Grandpa thinks there's a duppy in the house."

John started making shadow puppets. "Really?"

"Yeah. He poured our rice all over our kitchen and outside."

John's eyebrows popped up. "What for?"

I'd asked Dad that very question the next day. "To keep the duppies away," I said.

"Rice?"

"If duppies find rice around the house, they have to count every grain before they can go inside."

"You think they really *have* to count each grain?" Now John made a dog with his fingers, and the dog grew and shrank against the trunk.

"Well, that's what Dad says," I said, trying to ignore a twisting feeling inside me. "And it's best to put a lot of rice outside since duppies aren't too smart and can't count that high."

John snorted.

"They can only count up to nine before they get confused and have to start all over again at one," I said. "They'll never get in the house because they'll be stuck outside counting."

"Only up to nine?" John asked, with a strange smile on his face.

I didn't say anything.

A glint jumped into John's eyes. "So if I come over in a white sheet and start making wailing noises, he'll freak out, right?"

I sucked in my breath. "You wouldn't do that."

John laughed.

I tugged at a lock of my hair. "Grandpa's not that bad."

"Oh? He spits at guests to make them feel at home?"

"He usually stays in his room. I don't know what's wrong with him," I insisted, but I knew I was sounding like my parents just then, making excuses for Grandpa. While I didn't really want to defend Grandpa, I definitely didn't want John to say disrespectful things about him, even if they were true. But I was getting jumbled up inside. Was it wrong for all this anger to be stalking around the house, crouching in the corners? Was I wrong to make excuses for it?

"You're really uptight, you know that, Jewel?" John was saying.

My face scrunched up, I could feel it. "What do you mean?"

"You've got so many thoughts in your head you could live up there." John jabbed one of his fingers at my forehead. "Sometimes you just need to chill out. Relax, you know?"

I stared at him. I liked living in my head.

"And I have a feeling it runs in your family," John said. "I can't imagine your grandpa letting loose." He snorted. "Anyway, sheet or no sheet, I'll stop by your place tomorrow. Maybe he'll be there."

I froze. "And then what?"

John grinned. "And then I'll talk with him. Look, Jewel, if I'm going to be hanging at your house, I don't want to be chased away every time," he said, his voice as confident as a slab of granite. "I want us to be okay, you know? It's not right that he goes around trying to scare people."

A thrill of terror and excitement shot through me when he said that. I tried to imagine what Grandpa would do a second time around, and nothing I could think of made me feel very good. We ducked out of Event Horizon and made our way back to the road. Usually, when I'm walking along the road at night, I talk to the stars as they unfurl above me. Right then, though, I barely noticed them.

John decided to stop by without a sheet. I breathed a sigh of relief when I opened the door and saw him in shorts and a T-shirt.

"Is he here?" John asked as I let him in.

"I think so," I said. I had picked up the house a little, just for him, and everything was quiet and clean. Sunlight made the kitchen and dining room glow golden. The cool morning air had long gone.

"Where is he?" John whispered.

I shrugged. "Probably in his bedroom," I said in a low voice, nodding to his shut door. "He's always there."

"What does he do in there?"

"No idea," I said, fidgeting. I took an apple off our table and polished it.

John looked at me. "Seriously? You have *no idea* what he does?"

I used to think a lot about what he did in his room, since we share a wall. But I never heard anything coming from his room. Not one sound. Not ever. "I think he reads a lot,"

I said. "Sleeps. Maybe he writes letters back to his family in Jamaica."

John shot me a look. "Sleeps and writes letters? If I did that every day, I'd spit at people too." He took a step toward the hallway where our three bedrooms were.

I grabbed his arm. "Wait. You want a glass of water? Something to drink?" I asked.

John's eyes twinkled. "Nope."

He yanked his arm back and quietly walked down the hallway toward Grandpa's room. John raised his arm to knock on the door.

I sucked in my breath. A part of me wanted to run at John and pull him out of the house, away from Grandpa and the never-ending silence, but my feet stayed planted like a cottonwood tree. I couldn't stop him even if I wanted to, but then I realized that I didn't want to stop him. Not really. Not if John was going to do this so things would be okay when he'd come over. And I had to admit I was curious to see how John would talk to Grandpa without being afraid.

Still, if Grandpa did something to John, would I stop him? *Could* I stop him?

John's knuckles rapped against Grandpa's door.

Silence. Nothing.

John knocked again.

Grandpa had been so angry lately: first when he saw John and then that night at dinner, with the rice. I wasn't sure what he would do if he got angry again.

John looked at me and his eyes crinkled with an inside smile. He reached for the doorknob.

My hand shot out and grabbed his arm. I didn't even think about it, it happened so fast. But that didn't stop John from opening Grandpa's door. He peeked inside.

"Dang it," he said in his normal voice, but it seemed so loud that I jumped back a little. "He's not here."

I let out a breath, and the earth seemed to breathe again too. But my stomach stayed knotted up. "That's strange," I said. "He's almost always here."

John raised an eyebrow. "Or so you think." He opened the door wider. "Huh. A neat freak. I knew it."

John was going to go into Grandpa's room all the way when I pulled him back and led him down the hall. It just didn't seem right for John to be poking around. "He almost never comes out of his room," I said. "He likes staying in there," I added.

"Uh-huh." John stopped in the living room when he saw the family pictures hanging on our wall. They'd been up there so long, untouched and unmoved, that I couldn't remember the last time I'd actually looked at them. John was up close staring at them, staring like they were saying something, whispering right in his ear.

I squirmed. "What is it?"

He looked at me, then back at the pictures, then back at me. "You look like him."

"Huh?"

"Your brother."

I bit my bottom lip.

"You look like your parents, too."

I shook my head. "No, I don't. My hair isn't like either one of theirs." Mom's hair was thick and smooth, like water running over her shoulders. Dad's was wiry. Mine was an explosion of frizz with an occasional spiral.

John examined my face. "Your forehead. That's your mom's. And your chin."

"Really?" It felt strange to hear that I look like my parents. I'm always told I look nothing like them.

"And you had a dog?" John said, nodding at the little Xolo dog that was perched on a ledge between the pictures.

I blushed. "No, that's a Xolo dog."

"A Sho-low what?"

"A Xolo dog. Short for Xoloitzcuintli," I said, pronouncing it all slow and drawn out, *Sho-low-eats-queent-lay.* "They're ancient Mexican dogs that protected the king from evil spirits. They were even buried with the king to help guide him in the afterlife."

John peered at the dog. "Evil spirits? Cool."

I nodded. "So we keep a Xolo dog by the pictures of our family so it can protect us." I didn't mention that traditionally, Xolo dogs were usually kept by the doorway of the house, not by the family pictures. We weren't an entirely Mexican family, though, only partway, so I suppose that meant we could do things differently.

"Interesting," John said. He turned to look at another picture on the wall. "Who's she?"

"Granny. She died when I was young."

John studied her picture, the one where she was standing at the top of a hill, her crisp, white dress blowing in the wind. Grandpa had taken her picture way back, when things were right. Grandpa must have been really different, because she and Grandpa were really happy together. They'd take sunset walks along County Line Road, and they'd dance a lot in the living room too. Dad, Mom, Grandpa, Granny, all in one house, kicking it up. That always makes me feel strange, thinking about that.

John was still looking at Granny's picture. "There's something about her I can't put my finger on," he said. I was surprised at how intensely he was peering at it. Then he shook his head. "Wow. She looks tough."

I gave John a quizzical look.

"Like a 'Don't mess with me' kind of lady," John said, scratching behind his neck.

I shrugged. "I never knew her."

"You have her eyes," he said.

My throat got tight. How could he see all these other people in me?

"I don't have any pictures of Mom's family," I said, but I wished I did, so he could see them in me too. "I don't know anything about that entire side."

"Yeah, well, I don't know anything about anyone in my family," John shot back. I thought he was going to say something else, but he pressed his lips together tight.

I almost forgot John was adopted. I used to wonder if my parents secretly stole me away from somewhere. When we go out people look at my parents, then at me, and ask tentatively, "Is this your daughter?"—as if I were a neighbor girl or a complete stranger kid tagging along. And we always have to say, "Yes." Some families never have to say anything—their bodies shout out the answer for them: the color of the hair, the shape of the nose, the curve of the eyes. My body doesn't shout out that I belong to my parents; it only whispers.

But John's body doesn't even whisper.

"What's it like, at home?" I asked.

He didn't look at me. "I hate them."

I was startled. I would never say that about my family, even if I really, really felt it. "Why?" I asked.

John kept staring at our wall of family pictures. "It's not like they're even my family," he said. His eyes went back and forth from one to the other, and then to the Xolo dog, always returning to Granny's picture.

My fingers played with the insides of my pockets. "What do you know about your real parents?"

He finally ripped his eyes from the photos and turned to me. "Well, they were black." John's words were dry, sarcastic. "But I figured that one out by myself."

"You've never met them?"

He turned to me. "You've never heard about closed adoptions?"

I shook my head.

"Well, there are open adoptions and closed adoptions. With open adoptions, you know your birth parents' names, where they live, and maybe even visit them once in a while. With closed adoptions, you know your birth mother's age and race. That's it." John's lips twitched.

"How old is she?" I asked cautiously.

"Twenty-nine." The words stuck in his throat. "There. Now you know everything that I do."

If I were John, I'd stare down every twenty-nine-year-old-seeming black woman I met and wonder if she was my birth mother. No wonder John was so courageous. The odds of finding her were awful.

But when I glanced at him, John didn't look all that courageous. Just the opposite.

I didn't want him looking at those pictures anymore. I drew him into the dining room. "Dad was really impressed with my weeding," I said, "but he mentioned only the areas that you pulled up."

A smile crept into John's eyes. "Those were some massive weeds."

"Yeah," I said. "Dad forgets about weeding until they get huge." Little beads of sweat had gathered on John's nose. "Sorry we don't have an air conditioner," I said.

He shrugged. "I don't mind it. Air conditioners are fake. We should be able to handle light beams that come at us from some ninety-three million miles away."

I got us some ice water, pulled out two beef patties from the freezer, and heated them in the microwave. As we ate, the morning sun cast a rectangle of light across the surface of the kitchen table. John swirled his ice cubes around in his glass, watching them glint in the sunlight. "You know," he said, "the sun is here all the time, and yet most people don't really ever think about it." His voice was solid again, not like how it was when he was talking about his mother. John's shoulders relaxed a bit too. "Have *you* ever thought about the sun?" he asked me.

"It's hot," I offered lamely. I took a bite of my beef patty.

"Yeah, like twenty-seven million degrees hot. But it's made out of nothing but gases, right?"

I didn't know that, but I nodded anyway. "Right."

"So what holds all the hot gas together? What prevents the gases from flying away into space?" His free arm waved in the air.

My brow furrowed. "Gravity?"

"Yes!" John slammed his hand down on the table with excitement. He grinned a huge smile. "Gravity!"

I grinned back. He'd be a great teacher one day. I could just see him dancing in front of the classroom, his students shooting their hands into the air, begging John to call on them. Too bad he was going into outer space.

His eyes suddenly started sparkling. "The sun doesn't just have lots of gravity; it has lots of pressure, too." John walked to the sink to get another glass of water. I followed him.

"Pressure," I repeated slowly. I usually think about rocks.

Not about pressure and forces. But it gave me a giddy feeling, like my brain was growing and making these connections that I'd never noticed before.

"Even this sink uses pressure," he said. He lifted the metal arm. Cold water gushed out. "Your water tank sits above your house and uses gravity to drive the water out of this faucet."

"So our water pipes have water sitting in them right now, just waiting to be let out," I said slowly.

John grinned. "Looks like you get . . ." Suddenly he snatched the sprayer and blasted it on me. Frigid water gushed all over my clothes.

I screamed and lunged at John, half laughing, half shrieking. His grip on the sprayer was tight, but I angled the nozzle back at his face. John's skin dripped with water, his mouth wide and open and howling with laughter.

"You get an A!" he cried.

"Agh! You're awful!" I shouted, but the words were hard to say because I was laughing so hard. He kept spraying water right at my face, his free arm holding my wrist so I couldn't run away.

"You see? Water pressure!" he shouted.

I managed to jerk my body to the side to avoid another cold stream, surprising John, who still held my wrist.

The stream of water sailed past me and right onto Grandpa.

I didn't know where Grandpa had come from or how long he'd been there, but there he was. Right behind me.

Dripping.

I didn't know whether to laugh or scream or run away, and I think that just got me confused inside because I didn't do anything at all; I just stood there.

Grandpa's jaw clenched as he stared at us, his eyes sparkling with rage.

But John sure wasn't frozen. He looked at Grandpa and me and busted out laughing, holding his sides. The sprayer dangled in the sink, the faucet gushing out a stream of cold water.

I didn't know Grandpa could move so fast. He sidestepped me and lunged at John, whose lips were still in a smile from a sliver of a moment ago. Grandpa grabbed John by his T-shirt and started shaking him violently, his fists solid as rocks. John thrashed against Grandpa's hands, and maybe he was stronger than Grandpa thought, because at one point when they were fighting, Grandpa lost his grip on John's T-shirt and his fist crashed into John's cheek. John cried out and staggered back into the kitchen counter. Grandpa followed after him and tried to wrestle him toward our front door.

John's cry jolted through my bones. I ran at Grandpa,

pounding on him like an avalanche, beating on his back with my fists, and trying to pull him off John. Grandpa couldn't get too far, though, because the kitchen screen door opened and Mom stepped in, her arms loaded with plastic grocery bags.

She took one look at us, dropped her bags, and cried, "Jewel!" I let her pull me from Grandpa, and she stood between me and them, like a shield. "What is going on?" she cried.

"What are you doing home so early?" I blurted out. I suppose that wasn't the most intelligent thing to ask at a time like this, but it was the first thing that popped into my head.

"Stop this!" she yelled at Grandpa. Then she turned to John. "And who are you? What are you doing here?" she asked, her voice shrill and high. She looked back at Grandpa, who was still clutching John's shirt.

"I'm here," John said tightly, "because Jewel invited me over. And her grandpa punched me in the face for no good reason." John's free hands pushed Grandpa's away, and he stalked to the other side of the kitchen.

"Grandpa, is that true?" Mom asked.

Grandpa glowered at John.

"It's true," I said, feeling sick. "Grandpa punched him."

"Looks like Jewel's grandpa forgot about the whole *mi casa es su casa* thing," John replied, holding his cheek.

Grandpa's nostrils flared. His eyes were flint stones sparking as he stared at John. His breathing came in quick pants, and he shifted his weight like he was ready to spring at John again at any moment.

Mom stepped in front of Grandpa. "Enough. You are not to touch this young man, do you hear me?"

Grandpa sneered.

"He is Jewel's guest. *Our guest.* You have no right to lay a finger on him." She stared him in the face, her hands on her hips. I'd never seen Mom speak so directly to Grandpa before. "Leave this room. Now."

Grandpa glowered at her, then at John. He turned around, took a couple steps to the dining room table, and snatched the saltshaker. As he stared at John, he shook some salt onto the floor.

"Leave," Mom said.

The way she said that made me shiver.

Grandpa clenched the saltshaker and shook his fist at John with it. Then he stomped down our hallway and slammed his bedroom door behind him.

I let out a breath I didn't realize I was holding in. Water was still gushing out of the faucet, and I went to turn it off. John was rubbing his face, casually, as if he got punched every morning.

But I had seen that look of fear in his eyes.

"Is it bad?" I asked.

"I can't believe he hit you," Mom said, putting a hand to her forehead.

"Take a look for yourself," John said, pointing to the already swelling skin at his cheekbone.

"Oh, my God," Mom said, lightly touching the skin around John's eye. "Let me get you some ice." She crossed to the refrigerator. "Why is there water all over the floor? And your . . ."

Wet clothes clung to my skin. It was hard to hide a water fight. "John was teaching me about water pressure," I said lamely.

"Water pressure?" Mom's brow furrowed as she slipped some ice into a grocery bag, then doubled it over so it wouldn't drip everywhere.

John smiled a lopsided smile. "Jewel was asking about the physics of water faucets, and I was teaching her," he said. "And I think the lesson got a little out of control. We'll clean it up, don't worry. It'll be even cleaner than when you left it."

"I see." The skin around Mom's eyes turned soft, like when she wants to smile but doesn't. She handed John the bag of ice. "Rose. Call me Rose."

I was confused. Rose? Not Mrs. Campbell?

He took the ice and pressed it to his cheek. "I'm John."

"John?" Her voice turned thick.

John nodded.

I winced.

She looked at him for a good, long time. Finally she wiped her hands on her pants and took his right hand in both of hers. "I'm glad you're here, John." She glanced at me. "And you picked a great day for a lesson on water pressure."

I grinned.

It didn't take long for John and Mom to hit it off. She sat the two of us down at the kitchen table and brought us iced tea and even suddenly appeared with those expensive packaged cookies that were her favorite.

"When did you get to Caledonia?" she asked him, pushing the plate of cookies in his direction.

"Just a couple weeks ago. I'm visiting my uncle Tim for a while."

Mom's brow furrowed. "Tim McLaren?" She was too polite to mention that Mr. McLaren was white.

"Yup," John said, sipping his iced tea. He turned his face slightly toward our oscillating fan to catch the humming breeze. "He's my mother's brother."

Mom stared at him. "Really?"

John smiled his moon-teeth smile. "I'm adopted."

Mom's eyebrows popped up in understanding, then furrowed, embarrassed.

"I don't know anything about my biological parents," John said, even though Mom hadn't asked any question at all, "but my adoptive parents are great, so that makes up for it, I guess."

My jaw went slack. His anger was completely gone. Where was that sheet of black ice that had slid over his face just a little while back, in the living room? Now it was as if his adoption were almost an afterthought, something that you think about only when you're too bored to think about anything else.

Mom was smiling like those ladies on the commercials. "Mr. McLaren's a wonderful man," she gushed.

I tried not to let my eyes get all bug-eyed. Mom doesn't even know him.

John grabbed a cookie. "He's okay," he said non-committally.

"Where do you live?"

"We're in Norfolk, Virginia. Dad's a university professor, and Mom works for an insurance company." He smiled, then winced and repositioned his ice pack on his cheek. "I have no idea what she does, but she works in the tallest building in town."

"Wow." Mom had her elbows on the table, holding her glass of ice water with both hands, her eyes dancing. John could talk about dung beetles and she'd be fascinated. I squirmed. Maybe she was being nice because she felt guilty for Grandpa hitting him in the face.

Still, she never looked at me like that.

"That's terrific that you have a great family," Mom was saying.

"Yeah, it's pretty cool," John said.

My back muscles tightened the way they do when someone is lying. Except I didn't know if John was lying to Mom or to me.

John grabbed another cookie. "They're excited I'm studying to be an astronaut."

I sucked in my breath. Another scientist. Mom was going to have a hissy fit.

Mom smiled. "With your interest in physics, I'm sure you'll be a terrific one." Then she looked at me, as if suddenly remembering I was sitting at the table. "Don't you think so, Jewel?"

I nodded, unable to speak.

CHAPTER SEVEN

MOM sent us outside for the afternoon. She told me not to worry about my chores, and when she invited John to join us for dinner the next night, she even smiled, which surprised me, since I knew she was sad. It's not like she never smiles when she's sad, but usually when she does it's a halfhearted attempt that never reaches her eyes, like something is plugging up her smile, stopping it from spreading past her lips.

Today, her smile seemed to fill up the entire house.

The last time she smiled all big like that was two winters ago; she had taken me to Caledonia's county park in the winter, the one everyone goes sledding down when it snows. It was a sticky, bright snow, the kind that burns your eyes with sunlight when the clouds go away. The hill had well-formed sledding paths from the big kids and seemed to stretch up for forever, and we watched the kids come crashing down, sometimes toppling over sideways, their sleds veering out of control.

I didn't want to go up that hill. Not at all. But Mom said to me, "Sledding is the best part of Iowa, honey. They don't do this in Texas." And the way she smiled when she said that, that smile seemed to warm the snow and slow down the sledders and somehow made everything, everything okay.

After that, we climbed the hill and she plopped me between her legs, and we swooshed down, laughing and screaming louder than everyone. When we reached the bottom, she raised her arms in triumph, then wrapped them around me and hollered as if the sky, the sun, and the sparkling light would send us right up the hill again.

And they did.

That was the last time I saw her smile that big. After that day, I tried so hard to make that smile come back, but for some reason she slipped into this sad Mom and nothing did any good. I made a snowman for her in the yard, and when that didn't work I drew her at least eight cards until the construction paper ran out, and when *that* didn't work I begged her to take me sledding again. She finally did, but it was a chore for her, like cleaning the house, and she waited for me at the bottom the whole time. It felt so wrong I cried when I got home. That smile must have been a mistake, I decided that day. In a way it would have been better never to have seen it at all.

So of course I didn't want to go outside now that Mom was smiling like the sun. But how could I tell John that I was afraid her smile would slip through the windows or the cracks in the wall? In the end, I told myself that Mom was smiling because of John, not because of me, and that I shouldn't hope for things I'm never going to get. When I left her in the kitchen, she was cleaning up from our cookies, humming, and it was all I could do not to dash back into the house and cling to her leg like when I was a little girl.

I tried to forget about all that as John and I ran through the fields again, which burned like an oven in the midday sun, and we didn't stop until we climbed up the hill to Event Horizon.

"You're lucky you have a cool mom," John said, once we slipped inside the tree. The cool air on our skin made us both sigh with relief. He gave me a bottle of water.

"I guess," I said uncomfortably, and opened the bottle. The water went down warm, almost as if I were still breathing air. His cheek was swollen; it would take a while for it to go away.

John caught me looking at him. "It's fine." His lips curled

as much as his cheek would allow. "It won't be the last time someone hits me."

"Really? What other fights have you gotten into?" I couldn't imagine John getting into a fight with anyone. I squirmed as I tucked my legs under me.

"Hapkido. I'm a green belt. You get hit a lot." He looked at me, and his eyebrows rose. "A *lot*." He shook his head.

"Hapkido?"

"It's a kind of martial art. I'm pretty good for a kid my age." He paused. "That's what my teachers say."

"How come your parents let you be in hapkido if you get hit?" I asked.

"They don't like it," John said, rolling his water bottle between his hands, "but they know I do."

I didn't know how you could like getting hit.

"Besides," John said, "when you have a green belt, you know you can take care of yourself. One day, I'll be a black belt."

"And then what?" I asked.

"Then everyone knows you're the best."

I picked at the dirt under my fingernails. I'm not the best in anything—not even close. Not in math class or gym or art. Even Mom is worried that I won't be anyone when I grow up, maybe that I'm not anybody now.

"I think your parents are cool for letting you be in hapkido," I said.

The happy look in his eyes flicked away, as if my words had smashed it to a million pieces. "Like I said, they suck," he said.

My throat tightened. "But I thought—"

"Look, Jewel," he said. His voice wasn't as sharp this time. "People only want to hear that you have great parents, that you never think about the life they stole you from."

My jaw dropped. "That they what?"

John looked up at the bright hole at the top of the tree. "How do I know that my parents—my *real* parents—wanted to give me up? How do I know that they're not out there looking for me at this very moment?"

I didn't know what to say.

"How can I call Jack and Susan my *parents*? They don't look like me. They don't even talk about the fact that I'm adopted. Or black." His mouth tugged on the sounds of that last word. *Black*. "They just tell me, 'We're all human on the inside.'" He snorted. "Like that's helpful."

"And since people don't listen to what you want to say," I said slowly, "why bother telling them the truth?"

John paused and looked at me, surprised. "Yeah. Just like that."

We both stopped talking at that point. John and I, we just leaned our backs against the inside of Event Horizon and took our time listening to the birds chirping, to the humid air filling up the afternoon sky. It felt strange to talk about things that mattered—not things like what I ate for lunch, or did I do my chores. I didn't want to stop talking about important things, so I turned to John. "It's like with Bird," I said. "I think about him all the time."

He nodded. "You don't talk about him, though, do you?"

I shook my head. "Not really. Nobody wants to listen either." I stood up and left Event Horizon. John scrambled to his feet, following me. I found a good, low-hanging branch of a maple tree and swung up onto it. "Just like my parents aren't going to listen to me when I try to tell them why I was hitting Grandpa," I said, looking down at John. The trunk was solid and the nearby branches forked gently. I got to my feet, holding on to the trunk, and moved to the next branch.

John was already climbing up. "They can't be mad at you," John said. "Your mom saw everything." He pointed to his swollen cheek with his free hand.

"I saved Grandpa's life and they were still mad at me," I said, looking for my next branch.

"Really?" John seemed impressed.

"So I don't know why they'd be happy about me hitting him." The bark bit into my hands. I grabbed the trunk, steadied myself, and stepped onto the next limb. This branch stretched up at a steep angle. I bit my lip. A part of me suddenly wanted to climb all the way to the very top thin branches of the tree, to bend with the leaves and the wind.

Maybe fly.

"Okay, they might not be jumping for joy." John was perched on the branch I had just left. We were almost at the same level. "I get that. But they can't expect you to watch what your Grandpa does and not get mad."

I didn't answer John because I was getting confused. He had a point: If I had done what Grandpa did, my parents would sure be mad at *me*. But somehow, I wasn't supposed to get angry. Grandpa's the angry one. I was the responsible one. Levelheaded.

But it's hard to be levelheaded and watch what Grandpa does *and* keep all these secrets about the cliff and the duppies and the I-don't-know-whats that make my skin tingle. Mom wouldn't be happy knowing about that because I-don't-know-whats aren't practical. Dad wouldn't be happy either, because he'd think I'm playing with spirits and things that shouldn't be touched.

I guess I don't know what they expect of me anymore.

John was swinging around to a branch slightly above mine, the last branch before the limbs got thinner and farther up. A chickadee peered down at us, chirped, then flew away.

"Besides," John said, "you were protecting a friend, right? How could that be so bad?"

My head snapped up at him. A *friend*. Somehow, that one word melted away the dark, swirling confusion in my chest. I might not be able to tell Mom I want to be a geologist or Dad about the cliff, and I might not raise my hand a lot in school, but with John—John knew everything about me. As a friend should.

Well, he knew *almost* everything. And what he didn't know, I wanted to show him. John might not believe in duppies, but if he could share Event Horizon with me, why couldn't I share my cliff with him?

"John," I said, hoping he couldn't hear my pounding heart, "want to go somewhere cool tomorrow, before you come over for dinner?"

He shook his head in disbelief. "Jewel Campbell, what kind of question is that?" He had propped himself in the forking branch and was scratching the back of his neck. "Of course I do. You and me, we go everywhere together." His eyes smiled back.

I nearly broke open with joy.

CHAPTER EIGHT

WE met up the next day at Event Horizon when the sun was high and blistering. We didn't start at my place, even though it was closer to the cliff, because Grandpa was out of his bedroom more often now, doing things to protect us from duppies, like putting out bowls of water and hanging horseshoes and red socks and sweaters right on the walls. I didn't even know that bowls of water could protect you, but the way Grandpa put them by our bedroom doors and even in the bathroom, I supposed they did. I felt bad that he was working so hard to keep a duppy out, but it's hard to feel really awful for someone who just hit your friend.

John and I walked along the dirt road that led to the

footpath, which led to the cliff. His binoculars hung around his neck, as if he wanted to look at things close, real close. A flash of panic churned in my stomach: Did I really want to show him my cliff? My circle? For an instant I thought about walking right by the footpath—he'd never know, the long grasses covered it up so well. I could show John the pond with the slime over it instead, and I could scoop some up and throw it at him. The look on his face would be worth the retaliation.

"Helloooo?" he said, waving a hand in front of my face. "Earth to Jewel."

I jumped. "What?"

"I said, 'Do you think I should bring my mouth guard or my helmet to dinner tonight?'"

I looked at him quizzically.

He pointed to his cheek, still slightly swollen.

My neck felt hot, and I kicked at a stick on the road.

John suddenly burst out laughing. "It was a joke, Jewel!" he cried out. "It's not your fault he's crazy. Besides, with you as my backup, we can take him."

John's smile was contagious, and I stood there smiling and staring at him, like an idiot, probably. Why wasn't John afraid of Grandpa like everyone else? Instead there John was, letting his laughter settle over the grasses, and the grasses bent as if his laughter were raindrops.

"Come on," I said. "The footpath is this way."

I did have to point out the footpath to John, but to me, it was so obvious I could find it in my sleep. Dad had first shown me the cliff when I was eight years old, even though Mom was upset when she found out where we were going. "There's nothing she needs to know about that cliff," Mom said to Dad. He pressed his lips together and nodded like he agreed with her, but he took me straight there anyway.

That first time the walk took forever, like the sun was stuck in the sky and we were walking and walking and would never stop, but then suddenly there was the granite boulder and then the open space where the ground should have been. The hairs on my neck stood up.

"Can you feel it?" Dad had said.

I didn't know exactly what *it* was, but the hairs on my neck sure knew.

"This is where your brother jumped," Dad said, and he suddenly put his hand on my shoulder, strong and firm; I couldn't move if I tried. He looked out into that open space for the longest time, and the boulder sat there and watched us, listening to every word we said, maybe like how it sat and watched and listened to the noises Bird made before he jumped.

Dad turned and said, "There are duppies here, Jewel." His voice was low, and though he'd talked about duppies before, his voice never sounded like that, all strange and tight. I suddenly felt like crying. "Duppies are everywhere, but they like certain places. This cliff has duppies, and a duppy is what made Bird jump. The duppy tricked him."

"Maybe we shouldn't call him Bird anymore," I said.

Dad shook his head. "I don't know, Jewel. Whatever duppy tricked him might get upset all over again. I think we need to keep his name Bird." But he looked unsure as he said that.

I shuddered to think about what that duppy would do if it got upset a second time. "Should we forgive the duppy?" I asked. Mom's priest talked a lot about forgiveness.

"You can't forgive this," Dad said, and his voice turned hard.

Tears welled up in my eyes. I wanted him to hug me, to tell me that everything was okay and that he was going to protect me from every duppy that ever existed and ever would exist, but he didn't. Instead, he took his hand from my shoulder and looked out over the cliff, and I felt coldness where his hand used to be.

"Are there good duppies here too?" I asked. I really didn't

care about the answer, I just wanted him to look at me, to remember that I was here with him.

"I doubt it," Dad said, staring off into the distance. "Most duppies are bad because someone has done something to upset them." Dad paused. "The one that tricked my son was very, very upset."

"Why?" I asked. "Who upset it?"

"Grandpa."

Dad didn't know it, but I snuck away later that day and went back to that very same cliff with those legions of duppies, those bad ones and good ones and I-don't-know ones. The walk didn't seem half as long this time. I went back to where the ground dropped off, and I leaned against the boulder—I was too short to climb it back then. This is where my brother died, I thought. And right when the duppy was telling him to jump, I was being born. I ran the tips of my fingers over the rough grooves of the boulder, and I couldn't explain it but I felt like I belonged there, at that cliff.

To be honest, I don't know if there are duppies there, or if there are duppies at all. But I do know the first time I snuck out and stood at the edge of the cliff, my heart was stapled to my throat, because I knew *something was there*, and it was very, very important. The earth did too; from the grasses to the boulder to the smudged clouds to the trees in the distance, they all leaned forward, sharing in that silent secret.

It's hard to explain what happens when you realize that something is even more important than what you thought was already important. When making Mom or Dad upset suddenly seems like nothing at all. It's like the universe falls apart. Or comes together. But that's exactly what happened that day when the sky suddenly crushed down on me, when I knew that something was there. That same something tugged at the fibers inside my chest and didn't stop tugging until I picked up my first stone. That's how it started. Within a month I found my eight stones, and I've added a stone a year ever since.

As John and I headed along the footpath, he didn't say anything—not with his mouth, at least. The swooshing of his shorts, though, and the way he dragged his feet along, instead of lifting them up and placing them down softly, like mine, was as loud as shouting. It felt strange to be leading the way, unlike when we hiked to Event Horizon. Maybe he was thinking the same thing.

My thoughts boomed through my head and before I knew it we rounded the field. When I glimpsed the tip of the boulder, I stopped, and John stopped behind me.

"What is it?" he asked, his voice low.

I shook my head. How could I explain to him all that has happened out here, everything this place means?

"There's a cliff ahead," I said. I didn't mean my voice to come out as a whisper, but it did.

"Cool."

An ugly thought flashed through me like lightning burning over the earth. I spun around and faced him. "Why don't you know about the cliff?"

His eyebrows lifted and he leaned back a little. "What do you mean?"

"Everyone in this town knows about this cliff. About my family."

"Your grandpa?"

"My *family*. Why don't you know, like everyone else?"

John shrugged, but he was looking at me carefully. Cautiously. "I'm visiting my uncle, like I told you."

"Right. But how long have you been here?"

"A couple weeks."

A couple weeks. Could it be possible that he didn't know about Bird? The cliff? That his uncle didn't tell him about his cursed neighbors and to stay away? I paused, and I looked at the ground and imagined digging a hole next to the goldenrod by John's foot, a big hole where I could bury these fears. If it was true that he didn't know about

Bird, then why would I tell him—so he could think we're freaks too?

"Jewel, what's wrong?"

I looked away, but the panic in my stomach settled down a little. It was too late to turn back now, anyway. When I lifted my eyes, I saw a red-tailed hawk circling in the distance, watching us. I took a deep breath and pretended to watch the hawk, but really I was telling myself to calm down. Finally, I looked back at John. "It's a steep cliff. Watch where you step."

We slowed as we neared the edge of the drop-off and then looked in silence at the land spreading out before us. I had never shown someone where Bird jumped. Everyone in Caledonia already knew, and anyway, I'd always come alone. My throat tightened. He's probably going to make fun of me, I thought with shame. This is what I get for trying to have friends.

I didn't know what else to say, so I said, "This is where my brother died."

John winced. "He fell?"

I shook my head. "He jumped."

"From *here*?" John looked down the vertical drop, down the millions of years of dolomite and limestone and sandstone, of fossils and things that used to be hidden under the ocean but were now jutting into the air, exposed.

I paused. The sun was hot, spreading thick over the land, the air heavy and humid. "He was five. He thought he could fly," I said. I wanted to tell him about the duppy that tricked him, but I didn't think John would believe me. Not yet.

"Wow," John said. I waited for him to say something about what a stupid brother I had, and how I must be stupid too.

"Poor little guy." His lips pressed sadly together as he looked down the cliff once more. "And you come here?"

"All the time."

It was then that John really noticed my stones. He stared at them for a long time, his eyes moving from one stone to the next to the next, so intently that I started to get nervous. "Did you do this?" he asked me finally.

I nodded. To my surprise, he didn't ask why. Instead, he walked around the perimeter, slowly, until he made a full circle. Then he let out a breath, long and slow. "You really are something else, Jewel," he said.

I didn't know quite what to say to that, so I didn't say anything at all. After a while, John started fiddling with the binoculars that hung around his neck. "You know," he said, "back home in Virginia, we used to have this tree in my backyard that I climbed every day. I was really good at it," he added.

I nodded again. Of course he was.

“I had a friend named Nick, and he climbed it a lot too. We did tons of things together.” John’s face shifted. “Two years ago, Nick moved away, but before he left he gave me his biking gloves. Afterward, I found this hole in the trunk and put them there, and I would sit on the nearest branch right next to those gloves.” John dug in the ground with the toe of his shoe. “In a way, it was like he never left.”

At first I didn’t get why he was telling me this; I was showing him my cliff, I wasn’t asking about his friends back home. Then a slow realization dawned on me: John wasn’t laughing. He wasn’t making fun of me. A deep look had settled in his eyes, like he had gone back in time and was watching me lug my stones.

“I like it,” John said, turning around and taking in the boulder, the trees on the horizon, the sky. “No wonder you come out here. I would too.”

I didn’t trust myself to speak. How come my parents, who I’ve known all my life, don’t understand why I come to this place, but John, who I met just a couple days ago, does? How can trying to make someone understand take more than a lifetime, and someone else less than an instant?

“What’s the circle for?” John asked.

I shrugged, trying to pretend it wasn’t a big deal. “I stand inside it, think about things.”

He peered at me. "Like what?"

I couldn't hold it in any longer. "There's something here, can you feel it?"

He paused for a long time, his head cocked, and I was almost crushed under the silence of waiting. Finally, he said, "No. Not really." But he didn't look at me. "Do you think it's a duppy?" he asked tentatively.

"I don't think so. Most duppies like to trick people, but when I'm worried about something, or upset, I come here and this place calms me down. It listens to me." I stopped. I was pretty sure I had said too much, and I looked at the ground. It was terrifying that John was getting to know my secrets.

"I like it," he said again, all respectful.

My eyes bugged out. "Really?"

He grinned. "It might even be better than Event Horizon. But I'm not ever going to say that again."

I laughed, and it filled up the sky. I couldn't believe it. He wasn't shouting that I was a freak. A dam burst within me right then and a deluge of joy poured out, and I wanted to share everything I knew with him. "I climb this boulder too," I said excitedly. "Want me to show you where I sit?"

John grinned. "Of course."

He was good at rock climbing, just like he was good at

tree climbing. I didn't have to show him my handholds or anything, and he kept up right behind me. I also knew the best path to take, since I started climbing the boulder when I was ten—that's when I had grown tall enough to reach the first good handhold, a nice knobby piece that juts out and allows me to stretch for the next one, my toes gripping the rock. Sometimes I pretend I'm a gecko or a superhero, and other times I climb just so I can be close to that boulder, so it can hold me. Now, I know that boulders can't really hold me—I'm old enough to know things like that—but if you spend a lot of time with a rock or a cliff or a river, you get the sense that it's not really dead, the way they teach us in school. I mean, my boulder isn't going to invite me to the movies or anything like that, but it does know I'm there, climbing it. It also knows when I'm upset, and it comforts me. In that way it must have a heart of some sort, even if it's in a way we don't understand.

John and I worked our way up to my sitting ledge, digging the tips of our fingers into the broad, rough granite stone. Climbing a granite boulder is a lot different from, say, climbing up limestone rock, which has tons of nooks for your hands and feet. Granite is much rounder, its surface like rough skin, and you have to be really good at climbing in order not to fall. My sitting ledge juts out like a cheekbone, carved out by the wind and rain over thousands of years and overlooks the cliff to one side, the land to the other. The ledge is, though, only about halfway up—the boulder extends nearly twice that height above us. The whole of it must be forty or fifty feet high, and it rounds to a gentle tip at the very top. Frankly, the boulder is bigger than most kids would want to climb, but John wasn't afraid. He was sweating, though, and I hid a smile. He didn't think it was easy.

My ledge was small for the both of us, but we squeezed in. Boy, did I wish I had a stash of water and granola bars like at Event Horizon, because wherever the sun wasn't baking us, the granite beneath us sizzled. John leaned his back against the rock wall as we caught our breath. "I was thinking we'd go to the top," he said.

I shook my head. "I tried a couple times, but it gets sheer and the handholds are really hard." I paused. "The view would be great."

John nodded. "It sure would. We could try it one day, together, if you'd like. But we gotta bring gear out here, especially water." John grinned as he wiped his forehead with his arm. "It's crazy hot."

"I thought you said you could take some light rays from ninety-three million miles away," I said, kicking his foot.

He stuck his tongue out at me. "I can. I'm just saying it's hot."

"Well, you'd be toast if it weren't for the earth's geo-magnetic field," I said.

John hesitated. "The geomagnetic field. Right," he said uncertainly. He looked a little embarrassed. "I've heard about it. But not much."

I grinned. It was my turn to be the teacher. "So the sun gives off a stream of particles called the solar wind," I said, leaning back against the rock, "and it would eat through our ozone layer and turn us into something like Mars. But the earth's geomagnetic field deflects those solar winds."

"Cool. Like a force field."

"Yup. It also helps us by making compass needles point north, and it helps birds find their way home." The moment those last words came out, though, my insides went cold. What if Bird needed help finding *his* way home?

John was peering at the red-tailed hawk with his binoculars. "You know, Jewel, you're really smart."

"Not really."

He shifted his gaze to something distant on the horizon. "Shut up. You are. None of my friends back home know anything about the geomagnetic field."

I didn't say anything, but boy did that make me feel good.

"If you lean over this way," John said, swinging his binoculars around, "you can see Event Horizon."

"Really?"

John gave me his binoculars, and sure enough, there was the grove of trees and Event Horizon poking above the canopy.

"That's so cool," I breathed. "We could send each other messages with mirrors, me at the cliff and you at Event Horizon."

John laughed. "You could just call me."

"We don't have cell phones." My lips twisted up. I hate having to say that.

His eyebrows scrunched together. Then he shrugged. "Sending messages with mirrors is way cooler, anyway."

We watched the clouds that were pasted in the sky and debated whether they were dragons or turtles or airplanes. After I had persuaded him they were dragons, we got all quiet, watching and thinking. Suddenly John said, "You can have them."

I gave him a blank look.

"My binoculars." He lifted them a little. "So you could see whenever I'm at Event Horizon."

"What would you use to see me?" I asked.

He grinned. "My bionic eyesight."

I didn't trust myself to speak. Before today the cliff was my secret, my hidden place where no one could find me; no one could follow me up this granite rock; no one could possibly understand what a circle of stones could mean. The cliff was the only one that really knew what it was like to, well, be me. With everyone else, I guess I had given up trying. And I didn't realize I'd given up hope until I was thinking all these things with John sitting right here beside me.

I had known better than to wish for the impossible, but somehow I got it anyway.

After we climbed down, I tucked John's binoculars in the dry little crevice that held my digging stick. "Want to look for arrowheads?" I asked.

"What tribe?"

I shrugged. "No one knows. But arrowheads are everywhere. I find them in my yard a lot. Here too."

We dug around for arrowheads, and I was glad when John found a really great one. I convinced him to sleep with it under his pillow that night; maybe it would bring good luck. I was also glad because I wanted John to have something in return for his binoculars, and the cliff gave him an arrowhead for me. I won't forget the look on John's face when he found it too—we were digging by the base of this tree when he started whooping and hollering, and he even jumped up and down like a kid. It was like he forgot he was going to be an astronaut, he was so excited.

The late-afternoon sun was scraping against our skin like a hot knife when we headed home for dinner. "So if your grandpa thinks there's a duppy in the house, the rice didn't work then, huh?" John asked.

"I guess. But he's been trying really hard to get rid of it." My shoes scuffed the gravel road. Cicadas churned the air, loud and unseen.

"Looks like duppies are hard to get rid of," John said. After a while, he laughed. "Maybe the Xolo dog's taking a nap and isn't protecting your house right now. Maybe it ate too many tacos."

I laughed too, even though my skin felt numb. I didn't think it was that funny.

"I guess Jamaicans aren't the only ones who believe in duppies and stuff like that," John said.

"Why don't you?" I asked.

John sucked on his teeth and didn't answer for a long time. "If things like that are out there," he said, his voice low, "they don't care about me."

My heart sighed quietly. For all the duppies and banshees and ancestor spirits that crawl the earth, and all the angels and saints that hide in the holes of trees and sit on the tops of our roofs—not one cares about John? How could that be?

"Maybe the right one hasn't found you yet," I said.

"What do you mean?"

"Well, maybe certain spirits are drawn to certain people. Like friends," I added, feeling a little unsure of myself. "You can't be friends with just anyone," I said. I lowered my eyes. "I think. Anyway, maybe you just need to look for that certain spirit, or angel, or whatever." I tugged at a lock of my hair. "Dad thinks that when we're born, God assigns us a guardian angel to watch over us, all the time. Maybe your guardian angel lost you, with you being adopted and all, and is looking for you.

"And besides," I said, getting excited thinking about it, "the boulder cares about you."

John snorted. "The boulder?"

"Yeah. It was happy today that we climbed it."

John was quiet.

I shot him a look. "But trust me, you don't want a duppy to be looking for you. That's bad news."

"Bad news. Right." He paused. "Either way, it doesn't

make an iota of difference, because soon I'll be in outer space."

I winced. I hated the idea that one day he'd be gone forever, so far away that not even a spirit could find him.

I didn't get the chance to really think about this, though, because as we turned down our long gravel driveway, Grandpa was outside, standing by the front porch.

Waiting for us.

CHAPTER NINE

JOHN and I were still a good ways from the house, so far that Grandpa looked only a couple inches tall. Even at that distance, though, I could see that his arms were crossed over his worn, white T-shirt.

"For someone who never leaves his room, he really likes to come out and greet me," John said wryly.

"I've never seen him like this," I said.

John laughed nervously. "You just never see him."

John was right. And what's more, I had made it a point *not* to see Grandpa, even if he was in the dining room, sitting right next to me. Mom and Dad too, unless Grandpa needed something, which he usually didn't. I heard some people whisper that he was living among us like a ghost, but

I didn't think that was quite right, because ghosts are pretty obvious. Instead, to me, Grandpa was more like a thin layer of dust that covered every inch of our house. You just didn't notice it after a while.

That is, until recently.

I swallowed hard. "You sure you want to come for dinner?"

John stared straight ahead, in Grandpa's direction. "You think I'm going to run away?"

His legs took longer strides.

My heart was hot and sticky and loud in my chest. But as we got closer, the screen door opened and Dad came out. He said something to Grandpa—we were still too far off to hear the words—and then Dad took Grandpa inside the house, pulling on his arm.

Grandpa's head turned toward us as he went inside. Then the screen door snapped shut. I'd never thought of my house as being small, but right then it sure seemed that way, with Grandpa inside it and all. I wondered how there'd be any room left for us to breathe, much less eat dinner.

"It's Mom's night to cook," I said, trying to force my mind from thinking about Grandpa. "Her food's okay."

"Just okay?" John glanced up at an airplane crossing the sky.

"Let's just say if you see a flattened piece of charcoal on your plate, it might be meat."

John laughed. "Roger that. So if she serves charcoal, I should accidentally knock my plate to the floor."

"No. Don't do that. She'll just wash it off and give it back to you." I gave him a look. "Trust me."

John laughed harder, and before I knew it, I was laughing too. It felt strange to make fun of Mom, but in a good sort of way. I wished I could stay outside and joke around with him forever.

I especially wished that as I opened the front door.

Mom was in the kitchen, with a couple of pots boiling on the stove. A bizarre, sweltering smell filled the kitchen. My stomach twisted with embarrassment, and I shot John a *See I told you so* look. He was grinning at Mom.

"Hey, Rose," he said. "This smells great."

"It's a new recipe," Mom said. She had changed from her work clothes into shorts and a T-shirt and knotted her hair up on her head. "It's called Reservation Chicken."

"Reservation Chicken?" I asked.

"It's something where you reserve the juices for the sauce," she replied assuredly.

The chicken on the stove was boiling like it was going to explode any minute. Or maybe lift off into the sky.

"Where's Dad?" I asked.

"He's with Grandpa," Mom replied. Her words were calm. Too calm.

I stiffened.

"When do we eat?" John asked. He eyeballed the chaos of half-chopped food on the counter.

"Soon. Let me take a look at your face," Mom said, gently lifting John's chin. Her lips puckered. She got him another bag of ice. "How about you kids set the table?" she asked. Then she handed me five plates.

I sucked in my breath. Five plates. One for each of us.

A table the size of a football field would still be too small.

Mom put the Reservation Chicken and rice on the table with a flourish. "I think this might be one of our new family recipes," she said. "It was actually really easy."

I blinked at the chunks of withered, hardened meat. They looked hacksawed to death, the way Mom had tried to debone them, and then ossified on the stove. A thin, depressing gravy oozed over them.

"This is great," I said, at the same time that John said, "Good thing I'm hungry."

Mom beamed. She stabbed a chunk and gave one to John and then to me.

Dad's and Grandpa's chairs were empty.

Mom glanced at where they were supposed to be, and the smile left her eyes. "So, where did you kids go this afternoon?"

It was strange to hear her say *you kids.* Jewel and John. She seemed to really enjoy saying that too.

John jabbed his chicken and stuck a chunk in his mouth. "We went tree climbing," he said.

"Oh, really?" But her words were measured. She doesn't like it when I climb trees.

"Yup," John said.

Dad was talking to Grandpa in his room. In low tones. Strained.

"Jewel, you shouldn't make John climb your trees with you," she said, trying to talk with a happy tone to her voice.

"She didn't make me," John said. "Not at all. In fact, I was the one who suggested it."

"Oh?"

"Yup. Trees are the perfect places to conduct tests on gravity," John said. "When you sit on the lowest branches, of course."

"I see." I could tell Mom was having a hard time deciding if she should believe him.

John's eyes landed on the red sweater that Grandpa had nailed to our dining room wall, right below the horseshoe. "Hey," he said. "Why is—"

The door to Grandpa's room clicked open. Only Dad came out, his bare feet heavy on our floor. He looked more tired than usual.

Mom turned to him. "Nigel, this is Jewel's friend that I was talking to you about."

Dad's eyes scanned John from head to toe, lingering on John's dark skin, then his cheek. He walked to where John was sitting. "Good to meet you," he said. "I'm Mr. Campbell." He put his hand on John's shoulder.

"I'm John," he said.

Dad's eyes widened. "John?"

That one lonely word hung in the air. Dad shot a look at Mom, as if to say, *Why didn't you tell me?* Then he peered back at John, his eyes squinty and piercing, almost as if he were trying to lift off John's skin, dig around, and maybe find Bird.

John squirmed.

"Nigel—" Mom said.

"Well," Dad said quickly, his voice unsteady, "we're glad

you came over." He sat down and scooped a heap of rice onto his plate. He took only the gravy, not the chicken. None of us looked at the chair where Grandpa usually sits.

"How do you like Iowa?" Dad asked, his eyes still lingering on John's face.

"It's a different planet," John replied, his eyes wide. A small smile crept onto Dad's lips.

Suddenly a sharp breaking sound came from Grandpa's room. Like the breaking of glass.

There was a long, awful pause. I looked down at my plate.

"Is everything okay?" John asked. His eyebrows were knitted up in concern. Or maybe confusion.

"Grandpa's fine," Dad said.

I took another piece of chicken even though I wasn't hungry.

"You know, we used to have a son named John," Dad said suddenly.

"Really?" John said, all polite.

Mom shot Dad a look.

"Yes," Dad continued. "I gave him that name. John."

"Nigel, stop," Mom said quietly.

I glanced at Mom. Her face was tense. Just looking at her made me all tense too.

A series of thumping sounds came from Grandpa's room.

"How many signs do you need, Rose?" Dad asked Mom. "What are the chances that John"—he paused to emphasize John's name—"could come here and be friends with Jewel?"

"Nigel, don't sound like a lunatic. The chances are pretty good, actually," Mom said. But the strange look on her face scared me.

"Would you like some more chicken?" I asked John. "Or water?"

Mom was still turned to Dad. "Just let Jewel and John enjoy their dinner."

I stood up. "I'll get some water," I announced. "Does anyone want ice?"

"I'll have ice," John said. I wasn't sure if he wanted ice for his water or his cheek.

The pounding continued to come from down the bedroom hallway.

"You are refusing to see reality, Rose," Dad insisted, his voice tightening up. "Just let me teach her so she knows about these things."

My stomach lurched. "Actually, it's okay," I said to no one in particular. Why was Dad pressing on like this?

John's head bounced back and forth among us like a crowd at a tennis match.

"Jewel needs to know about the spirit world," Dad said

flatly. "Jewel meeting John can't be a coincidence. At the very least, it's bad lu—"

Mom stood up and slammed her hand down on the table, and the table jumped with the force of her palm. Silence hung wetly in the air. We stared at her.

Only Grandpa's pounding could be heard.

"Sit down, Jewel," she said. Her voice was quiet. "I'll get the water."

I hadn't realized I was still standing. I sat down, feeling nauseous.

We were silent after that. The three of us listened to Mom lift the kitchen faucet handle, listened to all the built-up pressure that was forcing the water out and into our glasses. She came back and calmly placed our glasses in front of us.

John put his ice pack to his cheek. "This chicken is just great, Rose," he said.

Dad's eyebrows shot up when John called Mom "Rose."

John gnawed on his last chunk of chicken and washed it down with his water. "It would be terrific on the grill, too."

"Do you think so?" But her voice was still strained.

"Yup. With charcoal," John said, throwing a grin at me.

I burst out laughing. "With lots of charcoal!" I cried.

I had a laugh attack right there in front of my parents. I don't know what got into me at that moment, but whatever it was, it came out, and it came out loud and fearsome and free. And I guess it was contagious, because John, after his initial surprise, started up too, until we were a fierce duo of openmouthed, stomach-gripping laughter.

Mom and Dad looked at each other, confused at us. At me.

And to tell the truth, I didn't care.

John and I were useless after that. Tears streamed down both our faces, and we gasped for air so bad that Dad and Mom sent us outside while they cleaned up. I couldn't remember the last time I didn't pick up after dinner, but there we were, running through my sloping backyard with our shoes in our hands, well past Dad's garden, the grass soft and warm beneath our feet.

"Did you see the looks on their faces?" John howled.

"You're terrible," I said, my throat hoarse from laughing so hard. "Charcoal!"

John bent down, ripped grass with his hand, and threw it at me. I managed to stuff some down his shirt, and we had a grass war until we were good and sweaty, until the grass stuck to our skin and our faces and our hair, until the stars slowly winked to life in the dark half of the sky.

"What was that all about?" John asked after a while.

"I have no idea." A strange feeling clung to the inside of my skin. "They never argue like that, not about Bird."

"Look," he said, spreading his arms out, "I can't help my name is John."

"I know, but—"

"But what?"

I looked at him. "What *are* the chances that we'd meet and be friends?"

"John *is* a pretty common name," John pointed out.

"But still," I insisted. "Dad seems to think it's unlucky that I know you."

The words came out faster than I thought they would, faster than I could stop them.

John snorted. "What could I possibly do?"

The way he said that made me shiver. "I don't know," I said. "But Dad seemed really worried."

John turned away. After a long while, he looked at me. His face no longer had that strange expression. "What do you think your grandpa was doing?" he asked.

"No idea," I admitted, picking grass off my forearms. "But he sure sounded upset."

"No book reading there," John said. "You really don't know why he's so weird?"

"He was normal before Bird died," I said, ignoring the churning in my stomach.

But John was craning his neck to the sky. "Hey, see that? That's Jupiter."

He pointed to a bright star that didn't twinkle; it just hung there, poised and beautiful.

"Jupiter?" I said softly, looking up into the millions of miles of sky. I was glad that planets don't care if your grandpa doesn't speak, or if you have a friend named John, or if the secrets in your family are like the endless, layered strata of the earth. "How do you know that's not a star?" I asked.

"Stars twinkle. Planets don't. If it doesn't twinkle, it could be a planet or a satellite or a slow-moving comet." He scratched the back of his leg with his other foot. "But that's Jupiter, for sure—it has a reddish color."

The scent of rosemary from Dad's garden drifted over to where we were standing, the scent that was supposed to protect us from duppies. I wondered if Grandpa was hungry or sad because Dad had forgotten to bring him food. That thought surprised me: I'd only ever thought of Grandpa as being angry. Not hungry. Or sad.

John and I stared up at the sky until our necks ached, watching the stars rise through the blackness and keep their night vigil over the earth. When the mosquitoes got so bad all we were doing was slapping ourselves, John went home and I went inside.

The house was quiet, the TV off. The strange sounds coming from Grandpa's room had stopped. My heart felt full and swollen, though. It was just yesterday that Grandpa had hit John, though it seemed like eons ago. And how could John be such a good friend and yet be so ready to go into outer space and leave everyone behind?

It was then that I spotted something on the kitchen floor—John's arrowhead. It must have fallen out of his pocket, I realized as I picked it up. He was supposed to put it under his pillow tonight. I grabbed the arrowhead, put on my shoes, and slipped out the door.

The sky was never so big. I felt like an ant making my way over the dark earth as I ran on the finely ground gravel road, up the little swelling hill, and then back down it on the other side. I ran quicker than the mosquitoes could find me. To my surprise, I wasn't even nervous about knocking on Mr. McLaren's door at night. John would have just gotten home and would be awake, even if the others had turned in early.

But I didn't need to worry about that; their house was full of glowing windows. I guess they didn't worry about their electricity bill the way my parents did. It seemed warm and alive, that house. Filled with life.

I rang the doorbell, and footsteps sounded inside. I covered the arrowhead with both hands.

The door opened, and Mr. McLaren stood before me. He was taller and older than I remembered, with his thin hair cropped close to his face and lines running by his mouth, even though he wasn't smiling. I suddenly felt unsure of myself.

He looked down at me, surprised. "Why, Jewel," he said. "What's going on?"

My neck felt hot. "Um, I just wanted to give something to John," I said.

"John?" Mr. McLaren's eyebrows furrowed. "John who?"

CHAPTER TEN

THE next morning, I dug holes everywhere. I dug farther from my circle than ever before, hacking with my stick into the hard, packed dirt, making holes upon holes upon holes. My pockets sagged with pebbles, heavy with the weight of John's lie.

Or whoever he was.

Every part of me ached, in the saddest-kind-of-sad ache I could ever imagine, an ache that filled my blood and my fingernails and my liver. I didn't know you could ache this much. And I didn't know that Mr. McLaren's voice could lodge in my mind, anchoring there for forever those two awful words: *John who?*

The ache inside me took on a hard edge, and my jaw tightened.

How could I have been so stupid?

Plop, plop, plop. Three pebbles were for John's dumb mouth, that it could be glued shut forever. One pebble was for how upset and scared Mom was at dinner last night. Two pebbles were for my ankle, which I twisted on the way here. Ten pebbles were so that I'd never talk to John again.

I had a lot more pebbles to go. A lot.

I was thinking so hard I didn't even hear footsteps behind me. "I thought I'd find you here."

I jumped up and spun around to find John. My throat tightened. "I went to Mr. McLaren's house last night." It was an accusation.

"I know." He shoved his hands deeper into the pockets of his shorts.

"Your *uncle*."

"He is." John looked at the ground. Not at me.

"Is not."

"Is too."

"Stop lying to me," I said, my voice rising loudly. My fingers tightened around the pebbles in my hand. "He didn't even know who you are. Where do you live, really?"

"With him."

Quick as a flash, I threw a pebble at John. It sailed through the air, over his shoulder. His mouth dropped open and he looked at me as if I were crazy. I was just as surprised as he was.

"Go away," I said.

"Jewel. I have to tell you something."

"Go away!" I started chucking stones at him, one after another after another, throwing at him all the ache inside me. John ran at me and twisted one of my wrists with both hands, and before I knew it I was on the ground, my knees digging into the freshly upturned earth, my arm still in his grip.

"Let go of me!" I cried, squirming. Pain shot through my elbow and shoulder.

"I have to tell you something!" he shouted.

"I don't care," I said, and I squirmed harder.

"Shut up! My name's not John, okay? You happy?"

I froze and looked at him. "What? What do you mean?"

His whole face twisted up. "My name's Eugene."

"You lied about your name?"

His hands were gripping my wrist real tight, like maybe my squirming was tougher than he expected. "Yeah," he said after a long while. He didn't look at me. "I didn't mean to."

"Lie to me? What does that mean? And why would you lie about—"

The soft look on his face disappeared. "Who cares?" he said. He dropped my arm and stalked away. I scrambled to my feet, slapped the dirt from my knees, and stomped after him.

"What's wrong with 'Eugene'?" I called after him.

He spun around. His eyes were hot, angry. "It's the name of Jack's father."

Jack. His adoptive father. I didn't get it.

"She couldn't even give me a name." His hands tightened into fists.

"Is your *dad* dad named John?" I asked.

"I don't know!" he shouted suddenly. "I don't know anything, okay?" He turned away from me.

It was so strange to hear John, the astronaut and the best would-be teacher in the world, say that he didn't know anything. Of course, I knew he was talking about his birth family, not about Jupiter or pressure or quasars. But my insides knotted up like a gnarled tree trunk when he said that: One moment he seemed to know everything, and the next moment he knew nothing at all.

I swallowed, but the gnarled feeling didn't go away. "Were you home when I rang the doorbell?" I asked.

"Yeah." He dug in the dirt with the tip of his shoe.

I crossed my arms. "Then why didn't you say anything?"

"I'd have to explain things to my uncle," he said quietly. "He'd be so mad at me if he found out."

"Oh, but I wouldn't?"

"You don't get it."

He was right. I didn't get it, not any of it. How could he just call himself John like that, I fumed. I mean, I don't like my name either, but I don't go running around telling folks my name's Jenny. And anyway, even if he wanted to give himself a different name, why couldn't he have picked the name Sam? Or Tom?

I could swear the sun moved an inch during all the silence.

He fidgeted, looking at the ground, the grasses. Some of my pebbles that I'd buried poked through the earth. "Why do you bury stones?" he asked.

I shrugged, turned, and headed toward the footpath, away from the cliff. If he could have secrets, so could I.

"Look, Jewel," he said, stepping in front of me. "I meant it when I said we're friends."

"So what should I call you?" I said. The words were sharper than I thought they'd be.

"Call me John."

I cocked my head at him and gave him a look.

He took a deep breath. "Really. John."

"Uh-huh."

For a moment, he looked like a little kid. "It could be my secret name. I don't like being called Eugene," he said. "But

John? It's a good name. Solid." He struck his chest with his fists, twice, like a gorilla. I smiled. I couldn't help it.

"I like how I feel when my name's John." His voice was firm again. He stuck his hand out toward me. "Shake on it?"

I felt my lips pursing up. How could his name change how he felt about himself? But then I realized maybe that's what Grandpa was trying to do when he nicknamed my brother Bird. Maybe Grandpa wanted Bird to feel invincible. Soaring.

I took his hand, slowly. "I guess," I said.

But I wasn't so sure anymore. Not about anything.

When I got home, Dad was watching a football match on TV, the non-American kind. Americans call football "soccer," but it makes more sense to call it "football," if you think about it. Especially since American football players mostly use their hands, not their feet. Anyway, football is Dad's favorite sport, by far.

He looked really intent on the game, so I headed to my room to grab some paper and sketch wildflowers, but he said, "Where'd you go, honey?"

I stopped. "John and I hung out for a while," I said. But it was a lie. We didn't hang out. We fought. At the cliff, where I shouldn't be. And his name wasn't John. How many times can you lie with those few words? An ugliness crept under my skin, and I swallowed. I wanted to run from the living room and hide under my covers, I felt so ugly.

"That boy. John. I don't know about him." Dad gave me a look that spoke a whole lot more than the words coming out of his mouth.

"What do you mean?" I asked Dad carefully. Did he know about John's name? Then I realized I didn't know about John either. Maybe Dad was right, there was something funny about him. A part of me suddenly regretted keeping his secret.

"I don't like how he called your mom Rose." He grimaced and turned back toward the TV. "That's not right for a kid to talk to an adult like that. No respect."

"Mom said that's what he should call her."

Dad shook his head, and I wasn't sure if that was because of Mom or me or John. "She likes to believe that things like that don't matter, but they do." He gave me a long look. "The smallest things can have the greatest significance."

I had no idea what Dad was referring to.

"Just . . . be careful." He stared at the TV for a while.

"Having a boy named John around our family..." He sucked on his teeth. "I don't want bad luck in the house."

I swallowed hard. Could I be bringing in even more bad luck by calling Eugene "John"? Suddenly I wanted to talk. I wanted to talk more than I've ever talked to my parents, to ask them about Bird and Grandpa and the silences and to have these questions answered, once and for all. And so, to take away some of the pressure in my chest, I said, "Dad, what was Grandpa doing last night?"

Dad jerked his head toward me. "What?"

"When John was here. What was Grandpa doing in his room, making all those noises?"

I looked at Dad, and he looked back at me, and I could tell he knew I was waiting for an answer. His face looked scared, almost. Then it ironed out. "He was upset about some things."

"About what?"

Dad shook his head.

I stood there, waiting.

"We shouldn't talk about this," he said.

"What things?" I pressed. "Why not?"

Dad turned up the volume. "Not now. I'm watching the game."

That same sadness with a hard edge flashed over me, and

my eyes got squinty. I went over to Dad and stood between him and the TV. "What things shouldn't I talk about?" I asked.

"Jewel." Dad's voice got louder. Annoyed.

"If Grandpa's upset, shouldn't I know why?"

"Don't use that tone of voice with me," he warned.

"I want to know," I said, my own voice rising. I crossed my arms, and the same mix of feelings swept over me as when I was throwing rocks at John: surprised but powerful. I couldn't believe Dad wanted to go back to watching TV. *He's acting like I'm a stranger*, I thought, grinding my teeth. If Grandpa was going to make a scene in front of us, in front of my friend, shouldn't I know why? Why didn't I deserve to know?

At that moment, Granny's picture—the one with her white, flowing dress on the hill—fell off the living room wall.

There had been no breeze. No pounding. Just like that, lickety-splat, the picture fell off the wall.

Dad stared at Granny's picture, then at me. I was scared too, but I didn't move. "I want to know," I repeated.

Dad cleared his throat. "Grandpa thinks that John is a duppy," he said in a strange voice.

"John?" My mouth went dry. "He's not a duppy."

"The rice was for him." Dad pressed his lips together, grabbed the remote, and turned off the TV.

Suddenly it made sense why Grandpa didn't want me to go with John though the cornfields and why he was so upset when I did. And if Grandpa thought John was a duppy, then of course he would throw rice on the ground and salt on the floor.

"So that's why Grandpa marked the ground with an X when he first saw John," I said, thinking out loud.

Dad grimaced. "That wasn't an X, Jewel. That was the Roman numeral for ten."

A number greater than nine that would keep a duppy away.

Dad sighed. "Okay?" Like he wanted the conversation done and over with.

"But John's not a duppy," I said, louder.

"They can take human form sometimes, to trick you."

A shiver raced through me. "Really?" I asked.

Dad nodded.

"But John's not a duppy," I said again, but more uncertainly this time.

Dad ran his palm over his hair and looked away.

Then a thought hit me. "You said Grandpa was upset about some *things*," I said warily. "What else is there?"

Dad stood up. "No more." He walked out of the living room and didn't say another word. I knew at least one reason why. Talking about a duppy can only attract its attention and bring it into your home.

But we both saw Granny's picture fall. And that meant it was already here.

It turned out that the little metal bracket on the back of Granny's picture had gotten loose and that's why it fell. When I picked up the picture, I half expected it to burn my hands or start flying around the room. But it was just a picture, cold and dead. I was hanging the photo back on the wall when I saw it: a flicker of light.

I stopped. There was a coil of gold lying at the base of our wall, where Granny's picture had just been, nearly hidden in the carpet. A thin chain. I went over and held the necklace up, and it sparkled and twisted in the lamplight.

It was beautiful. The kind of beautiful that makes you go quiet inside.

I bit my lip. How long had this been here? And it was real gold, I could tell just from the gleam and the weight of it. Which meant it wasn't Mom's. The only gold jewelry she had was those earrings. And anyway, if it was Mom's and she'd lost it, she would have made sure we knew because we'd be helping her look.

I swallowed. Maybe it came from a duppy. And if it did come from a duppy, it wouldn't be too wise to put it on. I slid my thumb and forefinger down the gold chain, over and over. Then again, it could just be a necklace. Mom would definitely say that.

I opened the clasp and fastened it around my neck, feeling like a grown-up. I'd never worn anything that was real gold before. If anyone asks about it, I'll just say I found it, which isn't a lie, I thought. The chain slipped perfectly under my T-shirt.

I went to my room and grabbed some paper to draw, but I couldn't concentrate. So I lay on my bed, played with my necklace, and stared at the ceiling. Grandpa thought John was a duppy. So Grandpa was burning rosemary and hanging up red socks and horseshoes to protect me. And of course that's why he was really mad when I ran off with John: Who knows what a duppy could have done to me? Maybe Grandpa was right to be mad like that, banging on plates and spitting and even hitting John—since he thought John was a duppy. It's not like he could shout.

It was strange to think that Grandpa had actually been trying to protect me all this time.

My brain spun like the blades of the fan that was blowing in my room. Just then I heard a noise on the other side of the wall. A *thud-thud-thud*.

Grandpa.

I swallowed back the fear that suddenly coated my tongue. He'd probably feel a whole lot better if he knew John wasn't a duppy, I thought, chewing on my bottom lip. I had to admit it was pretty strange that Eugene had chosen the name John, and that John might look similar to what Bird would be at John's age if Bird had lived. But still.

And maybe Grandpa was tired of not being asked how he was doing, or if he was sleepy or bored or restless, or if he wanted to play dominoes. Or maybe I could ask him what kind of person Granny was, I thought. She died when I was really young, just a couple years old, and I didn't remember her at all.

All these thoughts nibbled at me, didn't leave me alone. If I decided to go into his room, he might get upset that I asked a question or two, or he'd just ignore me, as usual. Or maybe he'd close the door in my face. That'd be all right, I supposed.

I had never been someone who would actually begin a conversation with Grandpa. But then again, I'd never been someone who would throw rocks at friends or demand that Dad tell me things either.

My lips twisted up. I heard the screen door slam as Dad headed outside and into his car; it was his turn to cook tonight and he was probably getting groceries. Mom was still at work. It was just Grandpa and me.

Again: *thud-thud-thud.*

I sucked in my breath, gave my stuffed rabbit a quick, tight hug, and got to my feet. The little white oscillating fan hummed back and forth, and I swallowed hard as I left my room and stood in front of Grandpa's door.

Maybe he could tell I was standing on the other side.

I made myself knock and fought a sudden desire to run away. Then I opened the door and stepped inside his room.

Grandpa was lying on top of his bed and wearing old-style headphones, which connected to an older-style portable tape player. Listening to music. His arm was draped over the nightstand by his bed. He had been pounding out the rhythms with his fist. That's what the noise had been.

His eyes flew open and he stared at me in shock. He pushed a big button on his tape player and yanked off his headphones, throwing his legs to the floor to sit on the edge of his bed.

All the questions I was going to ask had vanished. My mouth was suddenly rusted shut.

He stared at me, his eyebrows crunching together in surprise. Like, *How could you just let yourself in?*

"Hi," I said. I scratched my wrist.

He frowned, and the skin pulled deep around the corners of his mouth.

"How are you?"

Now, there are certain times in life where "Hi, how are you?" is probably not the best thing to say. Like if someone's bleeding to death. Or if someone's stuck in an elevator. Or, perhaps, if you just barged in on your grandpa and realized that he didn't want you to talk to him, but there you are, in his space, breathing his air and his grandpa smells and asking questions that really don't say what you wanted to say, anyway.

Or something like that.

"What are you listening to?" I asked, my scalp tingling.

Grandpa stood up, slowly. For a moment, I could swear I saw the skin around his eyes and mouth soften.

"John's not a duppy." The words just shot out, like they had a life of their own.

The softness must have been my imagination. Grandpa shook his head violently and glared at me, like, *What do you know?* Then he clapped twice, perfectly hitting that angry, loud spot between his hands.

I tried to make myself as tall as possible. "John's my friend," I said.

Grandpa suddenly took quick, cold steps toward me and grabbed my arm. He looked right into my face, his eyes wide and dark, and pulled me farther into his room.

I gave a strange yelp and yanked my arm back, my breath ragged. "He's my friend," I repeated, louder.

Then I turned and ran.

CHAPTER ELEVEN

THE next day, the clouds split open and rain poured down. It was one of those all-day kinds of rains, the kind that sinks into everything, good and deep. I couldn't mow the lawn like I was supposed to on account of the rain, and I didn't want to be stuck inside thinking about Grandpa on the other side of my wall, so I slipped on my shoes and headed outside.

I had decided not to say anything to my parents about how Grandpa had grabbed me. They'd probably scold me for going into his room. And they would be right: What was I thinking? Grandpa clearly didn't want to have anything to do with me. He never had.

I felt better as I walked down our long, gravel driveway and deeper into the countryside and the soft fall of rain.

The raindrops were warm and nice and fat, the kind that splatter when they hit your skin. Dad says that rain walks water your soul, just like the rain waters the plants and the rivers. Although Mom shakes her head when he says that, she always has towels by the kitchen door for me when I return.

It's something special to go to the cliff when it rains. My circle of stones sits there, quiet and patient and dark-dripping, and the boulder, like an ancient friend, watches the clouds crossing the horizon. Sometimes, if you look hard enough and long enough, you can watch the grasses turn from brittle brown to green, right in front of your eyes. And my buried pebbles—well, it's just nice to think that they're being watered too and that they're turning into dirt again, drop by drop.

As I made my way along the wet road, toward the cliff, my mind wandered back to John. Eugene. Maybe, just maybe, by giving himself another name, John was attracting the attention of a duppy and didn't realize it. Just like Grandpa attracted a duppy for Bird. Just like there was maybe a duppy in our house. My pulse started racing thinking about all that.

I bent down to pick up some pieces of gravel from the road so I could bury those worries at the cliff when I spied a deer path cutting through the grasses. It was a faint, fresh path that the deer made last night. Before I knew it, I was trudging along, excited. Maybe I would see a deer nest, I thought. Finding sleeping animals brings good luck. That's what Dad says. It wouldn't take more than a moment or two, and right now a little luck wouldn't hurt.

The long grasses were bent slightly where the deer had walked, and I stepped on the slippery path as carefully and quietly as I could, my eyes open and ears straining as if I were a deer myself. Rain dripped from the sky and turned the horizon into a soft, gray mist. The path turned a curve before widening, revealing a small pond.

My breath caught when I saw Grandpa.

He was sitting by the pond in the full fall of the rain, using a mossy tree trunk for his bench. His head hung heavily in his hands, his back slumped and sorrowful.

My insides twisted inside me. I thought he was in his room. But by the looks of how his clothes clung to him, he'd been out here for a while. And he looked so openly sad, the way people do when they think they're alone. Like he'd been coming this way for a long, long time.

Hot shame swept over me. John was right: We just always *thought* he stayed in his room. And that he liked it. But obviously we didn't know Grandpa that well at all. He didn't look like the Grandpa I knew either, the Grandpa who throws rice and storms about the house and frowns awful and deep. How could he have all these knots of anger and sadness inside him?

I don't know how long I stood there staring at him, as if he were a painting, or a dream. A red-winged blackbird shrilled at me in a nearby bush, jolting me out of my daze. As silently as possible, I backtracked to the road.

I stayed outside for a long time collecting cattails in the ditches, until the twisting sensation inside me relaxed and the darkening sky started thundering on the horizon. Only then did I walk home with my squishing shoes, feeling quieter, my soul watered and growing. Grandpa's shoes were by the front entrance, but his bedroom door was closed; I wondered when he'd gotten back and if he felt better. The floor was dry, so he'd either returned a while ago or mopped up well. I was curious what he was doing in his room. Sleeping, or maybe listening to more music.

When I got to my bedroom, I was startled to find headphones and Grandpa's cassette tape player with a cassette inside it. On my bed.

For me.

It was reggae music, but to me it was a portal into another world. Slow rhythms popped heavy like heartbeats and settled into my blood. I listened to the whole first side of that unmarked cassette straight through. This is what Grandpa listens to, I thought as I lay on my bed, my feet bopping back and forth.

It was amazing.

And he shared it with me. I didn't get it. One moment he was smoldering with anger, the next he was sad and lonely by the pond, and the next he was letting me listen to his music. I never really thought of Grandpa as someone who had *feelings*—with him being all silent, I just thought his heart was silent too. But I guess I was wrong.

As I was sitting on my bed, I held Grandpa's old cassette tape player on my lap, and it felt like an invisible door was being slowly carved into our shared wall. And that made me feel pretty special.

I listened to the cassette as long as I could before I realized I was late to see Mrs. Rodriguez. I ran to my bike and wheeled over to her house, which was a ways down the road, in town. It was one of my days to visit her and pick up a tub of her salsa, which she always has waiting for me in the refrigerator. On the afternoons that I go, I think I'm supposed to keep her company, but I don't really know what to do. Even though she's old, she can take care of herself just fine. The dishes in her cupboard shake when she walks by, her footsteps are so solid.

Those same solid footsteps sounded when I rang her doorbell. The door opened, and a cool breeze from her air conditioner tickled my skin. Mrs. Rodriguez smiled broadly when she saw me, and her long, gray-streaked hair was pulled back nice and neat from her face. She was pretty, for an old lady.

Mrs. Rodriguez clucked and kissed me on the cheek, then pulled me into her house, an oasis from the summer heat. She was already heading to the kitchen, where the salsa was waiting. Sometimes she adds *arrachera* or chicken mole if she has any extra.

The smells in her house made me hungry, as usual. Her *molcajete* sat on the kitchen counter, its rough stone edges still wet with bits of tomato and onions and garlic, which had just been pounded by hand into salsa. I was salivating. I couldn't help it. The only time Mom uses our *molcajete* is to prop open the screen door.

Mrs. Rodriguez was still chatting at me in Spanish like a squirrel as she bustled about, grabbing plastic bags for me to carry the food home. I smiled blankly at her, trying to push down my discomfort. I mean, she knows I don't understand a word she's saying. Maybe she's hoping that if she talks at me long enough, one day the switch in my brain will flip on and I'll respond with smooth, perfect Spanish. Or maybe she's lonely and she needs to talk to someone.

Mrs. Rodriguez piled up the plastic tubs of food with a flourish, almost like a magician: Today it was cactus salad, *tinga*, and salsa. I nodded appreciatively as the tubs disappeared into the doubled plastic bags, which she then handed to me.

"*Gracias*, Señora Rodriguez," I said, with an overly wide smile that I hoped distracted her from my awful pronunciation.

She gave me her usual hug, tight and soft. Then she turned to the staircase and bellowed. I jumped back a little, surprised. Mrs. Rodriguez held my hand. *Stay here.*

A young woman stepped down the stairs, her hair long and flowing and beautiful. The curve of her nose was exactly the same as Mrs. Rodriguez's.

"Miriam!" I cried out, and ran into her arms.

Miriam was Mrs. Rodriguez's granddaughter and had gone to college last year. She used to babysit me all the time; after she left, my parents decided I was old enough to stay at home by myself. I missed Miriam something fierce, with the way we'd make *sopes* and *gorditas* out of Play-Doh and pretend to eat them or serve them to each other.

Miriam laughed as she swung me around. "What a

surprise, Jewel," she said, smiling. Her gold drop earrings dangled elegantly. "Abuelita didn't tell me you'd be here today."

I got shy all of a sudden. "Today's a food day," I said.

Miriam nodded. "Of course it is! You always come like clockwork for Grandma's food."

"It's really good," I said, blushing.

Miriam laughed. "Oh, we know that. You always come back for more, right?" Miriam said something in a flurry of Spanish to Mrs. Rodriguez, who laughed too, and their mouths smiled in the same way. Maybe it's because of the familiar aromas or how Mrs. Rodriguez looks like Mom, a little, but in that moment I feel like I belong here with them. Then that moment dissolves away and there are more parts of me that feel like I don't.

It's like at school. I used to sit with Daniella and Silvia at lunch, and they were nice and all, but when they got excited or wanted to say something in secret, they just switched to Spanish. Sometimes they mixed Spanish into their English and didn't even realize it, like how you don't realize you're breathing. Then I would just wait, letting the sounds roll over me, ungraspable. When the girls burst out laughing, sometimes I laughed too, which made them laugh harder.

But Miriam wouldn't laugh at me. Maybe that's why I

said, before I could even stop myself, "Have you ever heard of Xolo dogs?"

Mrs. Rodriguez jerked her head back a little bit. Miriam shot a look at Mrs. Rodriguez and then said, "Yes, Jewel. I have. Why?"

The plastic bag suddenly felt heavy in my hands. I looked down and stared at the pile of shoes by the doorway.

"Do they work?" I asked quietly.

"What do you mean?"

I wanted to talk about duppies, but they wouldn't know what duppies were, so instead I said, "Like . . . do Xolo dogs protect you from spirits?"

Mrs. Rodriguez started prattling away. She put her face right in front of mine and talked at me slow and loud, as if that would help me understand something important. But as usual, her words just danced around my head, tickled my ears, then slipped away. She huffed, frustrated.

Then she and Miriam talked for what seemed like forever while I stood there, my eyes roaming the terra-cotta sculptures on the wall, the small fish tank in the corner—anything but them. Finally, Miriam laid her hand on my shoulder.

"Jewel, some people believe in the Xolo dogs, but others think there's just a lot of folklore around them." She peered at me. "Why? Is someone trying to scare you?"

Miriam probably thought that some school kids were playing a joke on me. "No," I said. "It's nothing like that—"

"Well, don't worry about it, Jewel," Miriam said, patting my shoulder softly. Then she paused. "What a beautiful necklace," she said, peering at the chain that peeked from beneath my shirt. "Look at you, getting all grown up. You never used to wear jewelry."

"Thanks," I said. I smiled, but my face felt like plastic.

When I got home, Grandpa's door was closed, but maybe he was out at the pond. I wanted to run to John's house and tell him that I was discovering Grandpa's secrets, one by one: What he does in his room, where he goes when he's not in the house, and that he has a thick sadness under his skin.

But just thinking of John and his secret name made me feel all scrunched up inside. Instead, I took out my favorite pen and started doodling until I found myself grabbing a piece of paper and writing a note to Grandpa. It was strange writing "Dear Grandpa"—all the other notes I'd ever left him were quick jottings, as if I were afraid the ink was going to chase me down for writing Grandpa's name. But this was a real note. I thanked him for letting me listen to his music and told him that I liked it. Then I drew a little flower after my name, just because.

But as I was sliding the note under his door, a funny smell came from his room. My body tensed. Something was burning. I sniffed again. Rosemary. Grandpa was burning rosemary.

I paused at the door, unsure of what to do. A part of me wanted to march in there and scream that rosemary and rice are things you eat, and they can't possibly have anything to do with duppies. Another part of me wanted to rush in there and make Grandpa stop burning rosemary, just in case, I realized with a start, it would somehow hurt John.

CHAPTER TWELVE

THE next day I stood in the middle of my circle of stones. Cumulus clouds shone like clusters of pearls in the sky. The granite boulder watched, its shadow angled thick on the earth.

A weight had lifted from my chest as if an eagle had swooped down and plucked it away. It had been a while since I had stood inside my circle—I'd been too worried and distracted these days—but it felt like I was coming home. My twelve rocks watched me too, bold, proud to have me back.

After a while, I stepped out of the circle and walked right to the edge of the cliff. It'd been a while since I did that, stand at the very edge, my toes tingling with all that emptiness a half movement away. When I was young, I would stand right there and dare myself to close my eyes, but every time

I did I'd get woozy and open them again, real quick.

If duppies existed at this cliff, they should have pushed me off a long time ago. But they didn't. I'm not sure why; maybe because they were waiting for me to be older—although they didn't think that about Bird, not at all.

Or maybe they didn't push me off because there are good duppies here. Maybe the good duppies were protecting me from the bad duppies, like an invisible duppy war battling this way and that, with the bad duppies coming at me and the good duppies wrestling them back, and a young Jewel standing, closed-eyed, right at the edge of the cliff.

Or maybe none of them pushed me off because there aren't duppies at all. That way, absolutely nothing would ever trick me, no matter how long I stood at the cliff, even if I dared the entire universe of duppies to come and get me.

The clouds lined up in rows and got tinier and tinier until they blurred into the horizon. I closed my eyes and started to feel the familiar wooziness come on, but I didn't open them. Not this time. "Bird," I whispered.

The cicadas whirred in the air.

"Bird," I said again, louder.

I kept hearing the cicadas. But there was also something else. Then, suddenly, I saw him. In my mind's eye. He was big now, older than me, tall and strong and smiling. He stretched out his arms, inviting me into them.

Then he jumped.

When I was young I used to talk to Bird all the time, like how some kids do to their imaginary friends. Except Bird wasn't imaginary. He just wasn't around anymore, that's all. But it had been a long time since I'd done that. Sometimes when I'd imagine Bird talking to me, I'd put words right in his mouth so he'd tell me what I wanted to hear, or I'd make him tell me my favorite jokes, or we'd laugh at something the teacher said in class that day. But the way that I had seen Bird, I wasn't imagining it. I wasn't making Bird hold out his arms, all open and wide.

I *saw* him.

I buried a pebble that afternoon, but it wasn't for Bird. I guess part of me was afraid that if I spoke out loud what had happened, it wouldn't be true anymore. And the Bird I saw was so crisp in my vision, so breathing-to-goodness real that I couldn't risk losing him, not even on a pebble.

The pebble that I did bury was for Grandpa, because I felt like I had been carrying him under my skin and needed to get him out. It was strange to bury a pebble *for* Grandpa—usually it's *about* Grandpa because he makes our house go silent. This time, though, was different.

For starters, I wasn't used to seeing him. Before, when

Grandpa would come out of his room, he'd sit in the living room or on our front porch at dusk. He'd never really want anything, and we never really asked him anything, until I guess after a while he just disappeared, right in front of us.

But now, not only was he out of his room, he was out of the house, and he was sad and listened to music that gets into your blood it's so alive and believed in duppies and burned rosemary and maybe liked chocolate. And the way his face softened—just for a moment—could that have been the Pooba that Bird knew?

I grabbed John's binoculars, climbed the boulder, and perched on the ledge that overlooked the rolling fields and then the hills in the distance. It was fun to use the binoculars: I could spot birds' nests, tell the way the different trees wore their bark, and see the way flies looked all golden in the sunlight. I swung the binoculars to Event Horizon. John was there, his body about the size of my hand. I focused the binoculars, enjoying a giddy, spying thrill as I watched him. Then I realized that *he* was watching *me*; I could barely make it out, but there he was, waving at me, jumping up and down, and gesturing wildly for me to come where he was.

He looked so funny making big gestures like that. I laughed. Then I climbed down and ran as fast as I could to Event Horizon.

"It is not easy to just run over here," I said, panting, as I entered the grove of trees. Sunlight clung to the edges of the leaves.

John grinned and handed me a bottle of water. "You made good time."

"So what happened?" I asked, wiping my brow with the sleeve of my T-shirt.

"You'll never guess what I found," John said, his eyes flashing.

"What?"

John paused, looking a little guilty. "You've been rubbing off on me, okay? I was digging around in the dirt and found this." He shoved his hand out to me, holding something. When he opened his fingers, I gasped.

It was a Xolo dog.

"No way!" I said, smiling. It was similar to the one we had at our house. I looked at John. "You found it out here?"

"Yup," John said, all proud. Then he gave it to me. "It was right by the tree nearest to Event Horizon."

"How do you think it got here?" I asked.

John shoved his hands in his pockets, thinking. "Well,

someone put it here," he said. "It's not like it's just going to appear places."

The dog was a shiny ceramic thing, with a larger belly than the one we had at my house, but there it was, that little fierce face, that protective stance. "Maybe it's a regular dog," I said, despite myself. "Not a Xolo dog."

John laughed. "Are you kidding me? This thing looks like yours."

I had to admit, he was right.

"You should put it by your doorway," I said, holding it out to him. "It'll protect your house from spirits."

"The Xolo dog is for *you*, not for me," John insisted. "You guys believe in that stuff. You should take it."

"But we already have one, and you don't have any," I said.

"So?"

"So you should have something to protect you . . . like layers of protection."

"Do I look like I need layers of protection?" John asked, and he stretched out his arms.

"Just take the Xolo dog, okay?" I said unsteadily.

"Okay, okay," he said. He went into Event Horizon and brought out some more water, and wordlessly we walked over and sat beneath one of the maples. He took a long swig, emptying the bottle in one gulp. I gave him my bottle and he took it, tilted his head against the trunk, and closed his eyes.

"You know what?" he asked. His eyes were still closed.

"What?" I asked.

"I didn't always want to be an astronaut."

"Really?"

"Yeah." He opened his eyes and peered at the tip-tops of the trees.

"What did you want to be?" I asked. My hands started digging at the earth, under the cool leaves.

"A firefighter." He smiled faintly. "You know, saving people and stuff. Going back for the cat."

The moment he said that, I could see him running into the flames, his face fierce and focused. "So what happened?" I asked.

"We were on vacation in Florida. Disney World, the whole nine yards. And when we were eating lunch, in the middle of the fun, my mom said, 'Wouldn't it be great to work here?' and I said, 'Nah, I want to be a firefighter,' and she said, 'Oh, you want to rescue people! Your dad and I are the same way.'" John shook his head, his cheeks tightening. "For some reason, I got really mad when she said that. Like she thought they needed to rescue me from my birth mother. After that, we went to the Kennedy Space Center, and there was something about those spaceships going up and up and those space probes exploring the universe, never coming back . . ." He shrugged. "It seemed a whole lot better than being a firefighter."

I mounded my dirt into a little pyramid and patted the sides. Out of the corner of my eye, John's face sure looked sad, even though he wasn't saying anything about it. Suddenly something about what he said made sense. *Never coming back.*

"I always wanted to be a geologist," I said.

"Always?"

I nodded as I picked out the leaves and sticks. "I didn't always know it was called a geologist, of course, but I was always digging and collecting rocks and looking at cliffs." That last part came out by accident—I didn't want him to think I was crazy, thinking about Bird all the time.

John's brow furrowed. "It's like, that cliff is everything for you." He said it really respectfully, though, like he was talking about Jupiter's moons.

I nodded. Then I started another pyramid, trying not to show that I felt like a giraffe on a hilltop, all exposed. I was going to say I should go home when John started helping me. We made a pyramid city in the shade of those trees, and we built it much faster than I could have done alone, with moats and roads and bridges and even a stable for the horses. It was incredible, the way it sprawled with detail, like nothing I'd ever done before.

As we were leaving, I saw him drop the Xolo dog in a pile of leaves.

"You really don't want it?" I asked.

John shrugged, embarrassed. "Not really."

"Then I'll take it," I said, bending down and scooping up the little figurine. I wasn't sure if leaving the Xolo dog behind would bring bad luck, and I certainly didn't want to find out. Besides, having one more Xolo dog at home couldn't hurt, even though I wished with all my heart that John would have kept it. I didn't know if it was already bad luck that he tried to leave it behind.

As I walked home, I couldn't help but think about how John had more than a flicker of sadness in him when he said he was going into outer space and never coming back. As I got closer to home, my thoughts turned to Grandpa, how he was probably there, invisible and waiting. Two sad people. But why would Grandpa shut himself in his room like that? Why couldn't he just talk about what was bothering him so he could feel better? Well, maybe not *talk* talk but, well . . . express himself.

Grandpa's shoes were by the door when I got home, which meant that he'd returned. Mom was home from work too, going through the pile of bills on the kitchen table. She always insists on doing the bills, since she does the same kind of thing at work. When I see her with that big stack of papers saying that we owe money, though, she gets these worry lines on her forehead and around her eyes. I always know not to make her more upset than she is. The easiest thing to do is just leave her alone and be as quiet as possible.

But John's sadness and Grandpa's sadness were pressing down on my lungs, and I was bursting to ask Mom about all this. For some reason I didn't think she'd want to hear about Grandpa being sad, so instead I said, "Mom?"

She sighed, switched to another bill, and propped her forehead in the palm of her hand. "Yes, honey?"

"How do you make someone feel better when they're sad?"

She was reading whatever was written on the piece of paper, her eyes moving back and forth really fast. "Sometimes it's hard," she said, but I knew she was thinking about the letter. Then she took out her checkbook and wrote something on it.

I shifted my weight. She wanted me to go away. "What about John?" I asked.

Mom raised her head. My stomach tightened. Now she was listening.

"He's sad," I said.

"About what?"

A beat of silence.

"I don't know," I lied.

Mom put down her pen. "You just do your best, Jewel. But sometimes being sad needs to run its course. It can take a long time, depending on what it is." She paused, as if she'd suddenly thought of something else. But the next moment she was back, studying me carefully.

She eyed the dirt on my legs, my hands. "Go wash up, okay? You have leaves in your hair."

"All right."

"I'll get started on dinner soon."

My breath caught when I opened my bedroom door. Grandpa had put another cassette tape on my bed. My skin prickled with excitement. He was on the other side of my wall, probably waiting for me to find his gift. Did he want me to listen to the cassette now and thank him afterward, or the other way around? I grinned and slipped the tape into the cassette player.

Just as I was about to hit the play button, Mom knocked. "Jewel?" Her voice sounded funny.

"Yes?" I said. I pulled off the headset and tucked it under my pillow.

Mom opened the door. "I just talked with Mr. McLaren on the phone."

I froze. "You did?"

"I was going to surprise you kids by inviting John over for dinner."

"You talked to Mr. McLaren about John?" This was not good. Not good at all.

"Jewel, there is no John."

I made sure not to move a muscle on my face. "What do you mean?"

Mom was looking at me, her face a swirl of clouds and confusion. "What is going on, Jewel?"

I looked down at my hands. Mom wouldn't understand about Eugene changing his name—and after all, I did say I would keep his secret. Do I lie to Mom and act surprised, too? But if I tell her the truth, she'll be upset I kept a secret from her. Tears of frustration welled in my eyes.

I guess I took too long to respond, because Mom's eyebrows narrowed, and she stepped into my room. "I asked you a question, Jewel." She cocked her head. "What is going on? Where is John staying?"

"I don't know," I said. Even I could hear the guilt in my voice.

Mom crossed her arms. "What has gotten into you?"

A tear slid down my cheek. I shrugged.

"Mr. McLaren said that he was coming right over."

My head jerked up, sending another tear down my face. I looked at her with wide, wet eyes.

"Jewel Campbell, you're going to talk with Mr. McLaren, and then after that you're grounded to your room for lying."

Grounded. I sat there, stunned. I'd never been grounded before. But much worse than being grounded was the look on Mom's face before she closed my door.

It seemed like a part of her love had just flicked away.

I started sobbing. I couldn't help it. I was still sobbing when the doorbell rang.

"Jewel!" Mom called.

I gulped in air and blew my nose on some toilet paper. Then I trudged to the front door, where Mom was waiting.

With Mr. McLaren.

And John.

Mom looked just as stunned as I was to see John there. John stood next to his uncle, his hands so deep in his pockets he could have punched a hole in his shorts. When he saw my puffy, red eyes, his face dropped.

"Hi, Mr. McLaren," I said through my stuffed-up nose.

"Rose." His voice was stern. "I'm so sorry."

I jerked my head up at him, surprised. He was sorry?

"Eugene told me that he had cleared things up with you."

Mom's eyebrows knit together. "Eugene?"

"But from the looks of things, I guess he didn't." Mr. McLaren frowned, shooting a killer look at John. John shrank away.

"So he does live with you?" Mom asked.

"Yes. But his name is Eugene, not John." Mr. McLaren put a hand on John's shoulder. "Right?"

"Right," John mumbled.

"Oh, I'm so relieved," Mom said, her hands fluttering up to her face. "For a moment there I was afraid he was a runaway or—"

"It was a cruel joke, what Eugene did," Mr. McLaren said flatly.

"A joke?" I asked, my voice thin.

"Tell them," Mr. McLaren said.

John was silent. He glanced at me, then away. "Uncle Tim told me about you guys when I got here."

"Go on," Mr. McLaren said, exhaling with anger.

"He told me about, you know. Your brother. John."

My heart dropped and fell to the floor. He knew. He'd known about Bird and my family all along.

"And at first I thought it would be funny to pretend my name was John, as a joke."

My breath froze in my lungs. It was all a lie. The cliff, his questions—he was pretending he didn't know anything. And the way he was upsetting Grandpa, the way Dad thought that John coming to our family was a sign, the happy way Mom kept looking at the two of us, *Jewel and John* . . . all of this was a joke.

Grandpa had been right.

John *was* tricking me.

"How could you do this to us?" I said quietly. Fresh tears streamed down my cheeks.

Mom put her hand up to her forehead. "I think you better go now," she said, her voice cracking.

"How could you do this to us?" I repeated, louder. John cringed. A surge of anger quaked through me. "I hate you!" I exploded. "You're not John! You will never be John! You have a dumb, ugly name, and you're a dumb, ugly person, and you're not my friend!"

"Jewel!" Mom cried.

But I wasn't done. "No wonder your mother gave you away."

His face was crumbling right in front of me, but I didn't care. I turned, ran to my room, and slammed my door on them all.

CHAPTER THIRTEEN

AFTER Eugene and Mr. McLaren left, there was a soft knock on my door.

"Yes?" I asked, wiping my nose on the back of my arm.

Mom poked her head inside. "How are you doing?"

"I'm fine," I said. I pushed my face back into my pillow.

Mom came in and sat next to me, putting an awkward hand on my shoulder. She's not great at giving hugs or even half hugs; it's almost as if there's an invisible plastic glove over her hand and the touch doesn't fully go through. Sometimes she surprises me, like the day we were sledding or when she was so happy and smiling with John. When she does things like that, though, it hurts—a place in my chest actually hurts—because those moments never, ever last long enough.

"I'm so sorry, Jewel," Mom said. "I was fooled too."

I didn't know what to say about that. I was fooled at first, but then I was lying to Mom. Eugene was lying to us all.

"Here." Mom pressed something soft into my hand.

I looked down. It was a bunch of tissues. The soft kind. I pulled myself up, and we sat on my bed in silence. A pressure headache settled between my eyes.

Finally Mom cleared her throat. "You broke his heart, Jewel."

The world was caving in on itself. Like Eugene hadn't broken our hearts? Everything was so confusing, so awful. I ached to have Mom throw her arms around me and rock me to sleep like a little kid. But she stared at some unknown speck on the wall. "You'll have to work hard to repair the friendship," she said.

"I don't want to be his friend anymore," I said bitterly, and this time, I was mad at Mom. Why didn't she get that Eugene was a fat, cruel liar since the moment we met?

"I understand, Jewel. I really do. But I raised you better than to talk to people so disrespectfully." She brushed back some tendrils of hair from my face.

"He lied to us. He said he was John as a joke," I burst out.

"It was wonderful with the two of you playing together; he had been so nice. For a moment, I—" Her voice wavered.

The muscles in my back stiffened. "I don't want to be

his friend anymore," I repeated. I suddenly didn't want to talk about this. Not any of it. Not about Eugene or John or adoptions. I didn't want to think about how I thought I understood him or how I thought he understood me. My throat thickened. I wanted to smash his binoculars.

After a while, Mom got up and left. When she closed the door I hugged my stuffed rabbit and rolled onto my side. This was just a big, elaborate joke on my family. But then why did he look so . . . ashamed? Like he wanted to shrink into an atom. If this was all a joke, wouldn't he be happy that he'd tricked us so bad? For so long?

I grabbed the porcelain Xolo dog on my nightstand and turned it in my hands. I liked the expression on the dog's face— not happy, really, but a strong face, one that didn't seem to be afraid of anything, human or spirit. Maybe it had even known that Eugene was an intruder, in a way, and was protecting me by kicking him out. I don't know how long I lay there holding it, but when I stopped thinking so loudly I heard a strange noise. Raspy. I walked to my door and opened it a crack. There it was again, coming from Mom and Dad's door. I went over and stood in front of their room, my ears pricked up and open.

Mom was crying.

I swallowed. I hated seeing Mom cry. Or hearing her. And I didn't want to know how sad she was because now she's stuck only with me. I retreated to my room. There, I dug under my pillow and put Grandpa's headphones over my ears. "Mento music," it read on the cassette, written in a careful, curved penmanship. Grandpa's.

The sound was coarser, older; different, not really reggae. The drums and the guitars and electronics of reggae were gone, and in its place were sounds of wood and wire and the ends of saws. At first it was strange, a little boring compared to the other music he'd given me. But something happened by the time I flipped the cassette over to listen to the other side: The rhythms had settled into my bones, and I could feel the dark, humid winds blowing over Jamaica. It was a subtle thing, this mento sound, but it clung to my brain like moss to a tree.

I listened to the cassette over and over, and the edges of my sadness slowly washed away. I imagined Grandpa, maybe my age, dancing. Being happy. Palm trees standing proud like kings. Ripe smells of unseen fruit wafting in the air.

My legs hung over the sides of my bed, my toes twitched to the beats of the songs. But my feet wanted more. So I stood up, carrying the cassette player in one hand, and found the rhythms on the floor. Another song started. I could see the black, forested hills, the dirt paths crisscrossing the earth, the flicking lights, the stars above. I think my arms were flailing, trying to touch the sky.

The hairs on the back of my neck stood up. I opened my eyes. Grandpa was standing in my doorway, a soft look on his face.

My mouth dropped into an O. I didn't know if I was in trouble or not. I clicked the stop button and pushed back the earphones. "I-It's your music," I stammered, as if he didn't know.

His cheeks lifted, like how people's do when they're going to smile. I felt shy all of a sudden. "I like it. Mento," I said.

He nodded. His shoulders were squared to mine, open. I don't think he'd ever done that before.

"Thank you for sharing it with me," I said. I held out the headset and player. "Do you want it back?"

No, he was saying with his hand, waving it slightly. He pointed at me, then his ear. *Listen to it some more.*

"Okay," I said. I struggled to find something to say. I didn't want him to leave. "What's your favorite song?" I asked.

Grandpa thought for a moment. Then he took the cassette player and pushed the forward button, then the play button, then the forward button, over and over until he found the starting place for his song. Finally he pushed play and turned the volume all the way up so we could both hear the music slipping through the earphones.

It was a fun one with a wailing, roughened sound to it. I smiled when I caught his head nodding to the beat; his eyes told me he knew every note, like he was seeing an old friend again. His hand tapped against his leg.

I couldn't believe it. Grandpa was in my room, being nice and sharing things with me. We were having a conversation. Honest to god, it was as if the sun were exploding. You think it's never going to happen, but then one day it does.

I wanted to give him something in return, and at that moment there was one thing I knew would make him happy. Truly happy.

"John is gone," I said. I was surprised at how much my voice twisted up.

Grandpa sucked in his breath. Not really big, but I saw it. The song ended, the music stopped. The cassette was at the end of its side.

"John was lying to me," I continued. "His real name is Eugene, and I'm never going to be friends with him again." But even as I was saying it, I felt all hollow and weepy, because that was only the beginning of the lies he told.

Grandpa's lips pulled together, proud. He put his hand on

my shoulder, and I was surprised at how warm it was. Then Grandpa nodded.

The rosemary did the trick.

I was still on my bed playing with my necklace when our old Buick churned over the gravel driveway; the engine cut off close to the house. Dad was home from work. From my bedroom window, I could hear him gently click his door closed—he never slams the doors, and he doesn't let us slam them either. We have to always gently close those doors like we're piecing back together an eggshell.

I could hear Dad's footsteps in the kitchen. He has a soft way of walking, like he's not sure if the next patch of ground will hold him. "Rose?" he called. "Jewel?"

For the first time in my life, I didn't respond. My eyes were still puffy from crying so hard, and Dad would take one look at me and start asking questions. I didn't want to talk about Eugene. I didn't want to think about what he was doing at his uncle's right now, if maybe he was being yelled at, or if he was laughing his head off at how bad he fooled us.

Mom answered back, though, her voice muffled through their door. Maybe she was still crying, her face even worse than mine even though Eugene was my friend, not hers. A tinge of anger sprouted in my chest. I pushed it down, but just barely.

I lay in bed, on my back, listening to Mom's and Dad's voices. Not to their words—that was hard through two closed doors—but certainly to the strain, the shock. I felt like Grandpa all of a sudden, silent and forgotten, listening to everyone around me, knowing that they didn't know how they're sounding. For instance, did Mom realize how heavy she sounded? How annoyed? Did Dad hear the coldness in his voice?

The tones in their voices grew louder, harsher, until their door opened, and the words tumbled out.

"Get that look off your face," Mom said. She was standing in the hallway, right in front of my closed door.

"I didn't say anything, Rose."

"Yes, you did. I can tell just by looking at you. And for your information, Eugene has nothing to do with it."

I could hear them breathing.

"You know it does."

"I can't stand you." That was Mom. She was walking away, to the kitchen.

"If only you had—"

Something slammed. Maybe a cupboard. "Stop it!" she

cried. "Stop talking about your stupid, idiotic things that have nothing to do with reality."

"Will you listen to me?" Dad was mad now. "I've taken this long enough. This is your fault. You refuse to accept the obvious."

"The only obvious thing is I married an idiot."

A long silence.

I wanted to cry, but I was too afraid.

"I see," Dad said quietly.

"Duppies. Spirits. Good luck. Bad luck. Nigel, do you really think that any sane person in this country would call you anything *but* an idiot?"

"Rose, her picture just *fell off the wall.*"

Another slam, the rattling of silverware. "So what?" Her voice inched higher now, a taut wire. "Things like that happen all the time."

"No, they don't. You bring curses upon us when you talk like this, and I won't stand for it any longer. I won't." A thumping, like he was hitting the counter.

"You're an expert on curses, Nigel." Her sarcasm made me shiver. "Get over yourself."

"Then how do you explain Grandpa sensing a duppy?" Dad said, his own voice rising. "Eugene pretending he's John? Pictures falling? How do you explain Bird?"

"Don't you dare talk about my son like that!" Mom shrieked, and I heard a hard slap. I dashed out of my room and into the dining room. Dad's face was still turned, chiseled with anger. Neither of them saw me.

"Grandpa killed my son," Mom said, seething. "Don't try to put the blame on me."

I cleared my throat. They turned and stared. The kitchen clock ticked loudly. Dad's shoulders dropped, like his hope had ebbed away.

"Jewel. We didn't think you were home." Mom's voice wavered.

"I'm going out," I said flatly, and as I slammed the screen door behind me, my heart started shrinking. I could feel it.

CHAPTER FOURTEEN

I WENT straight to the cliff. It was the first time I went at night. Nighttime can be an uncertain time: It's when shadows turn into solid things, when trees you know change their shape and meaning, when spirits freely roam the earth. Dad always says that you need to be careful around dusk, and then really careful when it's completely night. If dogs bark for no reason or if a rooster crows in the middle of the night, it's because they see something you don't—most likely a duppy—and they're trying to warn you. Nighttime is when the spirit world gains power and we humans lose it.

When I was young, I was terrified of the dark for this very reason, so scared that I slept in my parents' bed until Mom made Dad tell me that duppies aren't *everywhere* at night—they only stay in cemeteries—even though Dad told me later he was saying this only to make me go back to bed and make Mom happy. Duppies *are* everywhere, but they don't necessarily bother you as long as you don't bother them. That's what he said, at least. By then I'd mostly gotten over my fear of the dark, except for at the cliff.

It took a while for my eyes to adjust to the light. The moon was a waxing crescent, a cool smile, pointed and bright, but the shadows were much longer and deeper and darker than I was used to. I left in such a hurry that I didn't take my flashlight, and the world was half hidden in the darkness, angled and cold and strange.

A breeze blew across the earth when I reached the footpath, and the grasses bent in a blanketed rush. I shivered. Usually I love the sound of the grasses brushing against one another. Right then, though, the sound made goose bumps rise on my skin. I grimaced, thinking of the ceramic Xolo dog, which I had forgotten to bring with me. Maybe I should go back, I thought. Dad was right. This is not a good place at night.

My jaw tightened. No. I had come all the way out here. And anyway, home was no better a place.

I stopped short when I saw my stones. They looked so different in the moonlight, a silver and glowing ring, aloof, not at all concerned with me. Like they didn't even want me in the center of their circle. I bit my lip and walked along the outside of the stones, pulled toward the cliff edge as if by a magnetic force.

The space beyond the cliff was invisible in the darkness, and the darkness was deep and dense, like maybe I could step out onto it, maybe it would hold me. I held myself back. This is the edge, I told myself, looking down where my shoes stopped. Nothing good would come by stepping out into the darkness, even though it looked solid enough. The only clue that there was a gaping hollowness in front of me was the wind, swirling and howling in the space beyond my shoes. Even the air was different this late at night, thin and untamed.

I shivered. If duppies existed, they'd surely be here, right now, all around me, waiting to trick me off this cliff. And if Bird were here, he'd be trying to help me.

"Bird," I said out loud.

The wind howled.

I clenched my fists. "Bird!" I shouted. I was surprised at the tears that were flowing down my cheeks. "Help us! We need you. Do something and help us!"

At that moment I peered into the sky, waiting for a shooting star to sail by, or perhaps the vision of my brother that I'd had, dropping down from the heavens, or perhaps even a night eagle, bold and daring. Some sort of sign. But there was nothing.

I buried a lot of pebbles that night, more than ever, but for the first time in my life my pebbles were too small. When I realized this I grabbed leaves and sticks, and when they weren't enough, I got the largest rock I could find—larger, even, than the rocks in my circle—and lugged it to my burying place. Then I dug and dug until my shoulders ached and sweat covered my T-shirt, until I could fit the rock in the hole I dug. But just as I was mounding dirt on its top, just as I was finishing, I felt all panicky inside; this rock was entirely too small, I realized, even though it was the largest one I could bury. I'd need to bury something like a mountain, I thought, and at that moment, something wrenched inside my chest and I just gave up and cried.

What do you do when your worries won't go away? When even the entire earth can't hold them? At some point, the wind quieted down and I slowly climbed onto the boulder, but I felt like a stranger there, alone and uninvited.

Dad was waiting for me in the living room when I got home. A reading lamp was on, and his favorite late-night

TV show had just ended. I took my time slipping off my shoes and rummaging around in the kitchen, trying to calm down.

Dad glanced up from his magazine. He looked the same as always, except with some stubble from not shaving. Maybe the fight had been my imagination, I thought, but then I'd be lying to myself. They never, ever fought like that before. They might nag at each other or get snippy, but they had been screaming, *screaming* at each other.

"You're back late," Dad said, stifling a yawn.

"Yeah."

"Where did you go?"

"Out for a walk," I lied. Blankets were folded on the sofa. His nighttime glass of water sat on the coffee table, next to a disheveled pile of magazines.

He saw me eye his pillow. "It's cooler out here tonight," he said.

Mom had hit him. Just thinking about that made me go all cold inside. And even though I tried to think of a million other things, I kept hearing Mom's hand smack across Dad's face, over and over and over.

"Do you want me to turn the fan on?" I asked.

"Sure."

As I crossed the room, I wondered how long we weren't

going to mention the fight. How it would be one more layer of things we don't talk about.

I was getting sick of all these layers.

"Dad," I said quietly, "are you guys going to get a divorce?"

Dad coughed. "No, Jewel—what would make you say that?"

Now that was a pretty dumb question, given what I'd heard and seen. I couldn't figure out how to respond to that without sounding disrespectful.

"Well, we . . . disagree sometimes. That's all." He took off his reading glasses and rubbed his face with both hands. "We're fine, honey. Give it a day or two."

I sighed inside and made my way to my bedroom. No light came from under my parents' door, but I wondered if Mom was still awake, lying in the darkness. Maybe Grandpa was doing the same thing. How funny would it be, I thought, if there was an entire house of people in the dark, lying on their beds and thinking about each other.

I went to my room and watched the stars from my bedroom window. They had moved only slightly from when I was at the cliff. A burst of light flashed across the sky, bright and daring. My breath caught. Was it a comet? Or a meteorite? I bit my lip. Eugene would know what it was. If he had been here, I wouldn't even have to ask him. He'd just blurt it out and my brain would grow smarter, simple as that.

But of course it wasn't as simple as that anymore, since I was never going to talk with Eugene again.

I sighed, and an awful feeling clung to the insides of my skin. Far above, those stars still glistened, dripped with light, from way back in time. I wish I could go back in time, I thought, hugging my stuffed rabbit. I'm not sure what I'd do, but it'd be better somehow. John—when he was a John—and I would climb trees and laugh until our sides ached. I would still have a friend. Instead, the stars hovered over a person named Eugene who lied to us all. I tossed in bed for a long time that night, and the last things that flitted through my mind before I fell asleep were my circle, my boulder, my pebbles—all my rocks sitting under the dark, forever sky.

Dad had been sleeping on the couch for two weeks when Mom decided she was going to stop cooking. For good. She made the announcement at dinner. The four of us were seated around the table, the moths hitting up against the window screens. Mom had put spaghetti on the table, and we were slurping and scraping and chewing when I suddenly noticed she hadn't touched her food. Not at all. Instead, she sat with her back straight and watched us.

"This is my last meal," she said.

The three of us looked up at her. Even Grandpa. We waited.

"I'm tired of cooking." Mom brushed an ant off the table. "No. I hate cooking."

Dad wiped his mouth with a napkin. "Okay," he said.

"I'm sick of watching the sales for food, buying food, cleaning up after food." Mom's hand waved through the air. "Do you realize how tedious it is? How mind-numbing?"

"I'll cook, Mom," I offered, trying to act all calm. "I make great grilled cheese sandwiches."

Grandpa looked back down at the table.

"I don't think you understand what I'm saying," Mom said quietly.

Something in her voice made the hairs on my arms stand on end. I twisted my spaghetti around my fork much thicker than I could ever hope to get it into my mouth.

"Jewel," Dad said, "use your knife. You're going to make a mess."

"Okay," I said.

Grandpa's fork scratched against his plate.

"I have to go to the bathroom," I said.

"Jewel," Mom said.

My heart got loud. I waited.

Mom looked at us. "I'm never going to cook again." She spoke slow, like we were dumb.

"Rose," Dad said, "you already said that. We got it."

I wanted to throw myself at Mom's ankles and sob, *I'm sorry I disappoint you. Just don't leave us.* Instead I said, "We'll figure it out, Mom."

"Good," she said. She pushed her chair back, stood up, and walked away.

I cut my noodles into super small pieces.

"I'm cooking tomorrow," Dad said to me after she had left. "Don't worry about it."

"I can make quesadillas, too. With tomato soup. And omelets."

"I know," he said.

Grandpa chewed loudly, smacked his lips. I looked up at him and was startled that he was eyeing me. He nodded slightly.

"Should I talk with her?" I blurted out.

Dad exhaled loudly. "No," he said. "I don't think it'll help."

Dad left soon after that to sit outside on our front porch. I put some of the dishes in the kitchen, but when I went back to the dining room to get the rest, I found that the plates had already been stacked up. Grandpa was on his feet, helping me. He'd never done that before.

I blushed and gave a slight smile.

Grandpa pointed to his forehead, then to Mom's plate of untouched food.

My smile widened. "I would love for you to help me cook," I said.

Grandpa nodded again. I had understood.

Dad was right: He did cook the next day. But the day after that he didn't come home until almost eight o'clock, so I ended up making grilled cheese for Grandpa and me. And two days after that, when Grandpa and I were sick of grilled cheese, I started opening up cans of creamed corn and refried beans, all of which had been sitting in the back of the cupboard for at least three whole years. Mom was in and out of the house, not saying much, just nibbling food here and there. And I didn't know what Dad ate, but it wasn't at home. Maybe he was sick of grilled cheese sandwiches too.

The thing about cooking is, once you get something down—like grilled cheese or omelets—your mind starts to wander a bit. Even though it was two weeks since Dad and Mom's fight, my brain kept reliving their arguments, like a movie caught in replay. And while I hadn't understood much, I did know that my parents knew a lot, lot more than what they were telling me. And how could Dad blame Mom for Bird's death? We knew it was Grandpa's fault.

Grandpa didn't mean it, of course. If someone had told him, *Look, if you name him Bird it'll either attract a duppy or mess with his head and either way he's going to die*, I bet Grandpa wouldn't have done it. And even though there were those pictures of Grandpa smiling all wide and big with Bird, it was Grandpa who killed Bird, not Mom. But then Mom called Dad an idiot, but I know for a fact that Dad's a really smart guy, especially with plants and duppies. So maybe they're all wrong.

I was thinking so hard about how my family was falling apart that I didn't notice the thick smoke that had filled the kitchen. Suddenly, the oil in the frying pan burst into flames. I jumped back and screamed, and just kept screaming like a lunatic when Grandpa barged into the kitchen like a bull. He clanged a lid on the frying pan, smothering the flames, then turned off the stove.

Acrid smoke hung in the air. "Sorry, Grandpa," I said. I wanted to weep. "That was our lunch."

He stared at me for a long time, his eyes wide with alarm. After the scared look left his face, he shrugged and raised his eyebrows, like *Everyone's lunch is on fire once in a while.* Then he moved a fan to the kitchen to blow out the smoke.

When most of the haze had cleared, he opened the lid to the frying pan and peeked inside. His eyebrows knitted together; we were going to eat omelets again. This time charred.

"I guess I don't know how to make much else," I said, looking at my feet.

Air came out of his nose, the beginning of a laugh. His cheeks lifted again, and he turned to the freezer, took out some fish, and soaked it in water. When it was thawed, Grandpa fried up the fish with some bacon and onions and hot peppers. Then he opened up a can of ackee, a yellow, mellow-flavored fruit that looks like scrambled eggs, drained the liquid, and threw the ackee in too. It was kind of funny to watch Grandpa make ackee and saltfish without the saltfish—that's salted cod, all dried and leathery—but our grocery store in Caledonia doesn't keep saltfish on hand, just like it doesn't have Jamaican Scotch bonnet peppers, so we have to use Mexican serrano peppers instead. I was surprised we had a can of ackee, honestly—but then again, he did have to go digging in the back of our pantry.

While all that was cooking, he put some flour, salt, baking powder, milk, and butter in a bowl and kneaded it with his hands, then formed the dough into little balls the size of lemons, flattening them down just slightly. Then he threw the dumplings into a separate pan with oil and fried them up until they were golden.

The entire meal appeared in almost no time. I couldn't believe how good he was at cooking—much better than Dad, and way better than Mom. Dad must have known his father could cook. Why was Grandpa just sitting in his room and eating things like Reservation Chicken all these years?

Grandpa made just enough food for the two of us, which was surprising, since my family always made more than enough for leftovers. It would have been great to share some with Dad and Mom and show them how terrific a cook Grandpa is.

"Thanks, Grandpa," I said, patting my belly. "That was amazing."

The corners of Grandpa's lips pulled up into a slight smile.

"Did you learn that in Jamaica?"

Grandpa nodded.

"You should cook for Dad and Mom one night," I offered, jabbing at the last bit of ackee with my fork. "They'd be so surprised."

A sudden hardness came over Grandpa's face.

Then I got it.

"You made only enough for the two of us on purpose, didn't you?" I asked tentatively.

Grandpa ran his hand over the thick, short hairs on his head, his eyes flicking away. I sucked in my breath a little. I never realized that secrets could be heavier than a backpack full of bricks. Until now.

Grandpa stood up. He looked at me in a way that made me stand up too.

"You could teach me a thing or two about cooking," I said, trying to fill the silence. "It was great."

But he wasn't listening to me. He disappeared into his room and came back with another cassette. He gave it to me.

My smile reached from ear to ear. Grandpa made a twirling motion with a finger.

"You want me to play it now?" I asked.

He nodded. He looked a little nervous.

I brought the cassette player to the dining room table and turned up the volume so we could both listen.

To my surprise, there were no drums, no strings, no music. Instead, this time, someone was speaking. His voice was grainy, distant. "So here we are, on Valentine's Day," the voice said, low and whispering, "waiting for the women to get back from the store."

I looked at Grandpa, confused. He cocked his head, listening, his eyes sparkling.

The tape rolled on. "We've set the house up with candles and roses, and Nigel actually cleaned the bathroom."

"Dad, do you have to make a tape of everything?" said the other voice. Nigel. My dad.

"You bet I do," the other man said, and laughed. "Otherwise, how else would I have proof of how crazy you are?"

Then I got it. "That was *you* talking?" I asked Grandpa. I'm glad eyeballs can't just pop out, because if they could, mine would have rolled right onto the floor.

Grandpa hit the table with his hand, he was so excited.

"I like your voice," I said softly.

Grandpa looked a little embarrassed and rubbed the back of his neck. A slow smile spread across my face.

The cassette kept playing. "Anyway," Dad said playfully, "I cleaned the bathroom because when you clean it, the ladies say it just gets dirtier." His voice sounded younger, somehow. Or maybe voices just sound younger when you're happy.

"Attention, attention," the Grandpa on the tape whispered. "The women are coming up the driveway."

"They're coming," Dad whispered.

"That's what I just said, Nigel. Be quiet. They're at the door."

"Now who needs to be quiet!"

There was a thick moment of waiting, and then the guys yelled out suddenly, "Surprise!"

I guess Mom and Granny were pretty surprised, since they were yelling and laughing and talking all at once. "Mom! Show them *our* surprise!" Mom called out in a giddy voice. I was confused for a moment until I realized Mom meant Granny, and then I was doubly confused to hear Mom's voice sound so . . . happy. So free.

Mom's voice rang out loud and clear. "Oh, you men are just too romantic! Chocolates and everything! Now look at what we got you."

Dad and Grandpa started laughing. "Socks?" Dad said.

On the tape, Grandpa snorted.

"Your favorite color," Granny added.

"These are the finest socks I've ever seen, mi love," Grandpa said.

We couldn't get any further, though, because at that moment, Mom walked in the house, which was strange, since she was supposed to be at work. She looked right at us and didn't see the cassette player or the headphones or notice that Grandpa and I were being nice to each other.

That's because there were tears in her eyes.

"Mom," I said, standing up. "What happened?"

"What are we going to do?" She choked on her last words.

A hand flew up to her mouth. Grandpa stiffened.

My stomach twisted. "What do you mean?"

"Jewel Campbell, what have you been doing at that cliff?"

Grandpa's eyes got big.

My mouth dropped open. "I'm not—"

"It doesn't matter anymore, I suppose," Mom said, her voice wet and wobbly. "None of it does." Then she sat down at the table, covered her face with her hands, and went silent and still for the longest time.

"And what are you doing with a circle of stones?" she whispered into the table.

The world started to spin. "I don't know—"

"Don't lie to me." Her voice got thick. She looked up. "You weren't supposed to go there anymore." She paused. "It took me years to make people here comfortable with Nigel and his talk, only to have to deal now with you."

"But I wasn't doing anything bad," I protested.

Mom groaned.

"Really," I insisted.

"Well, whatever it was, it was too much for them." Mom swiped at a tear on her cheek. "Mr. Robinson heard that you had made a circle of stones. Jewel, I work for the town; have you forgotten that?"

Mr. Robinson. Her boss and the mayor, the man in

charge of all things in Caledonia. He was also a minster at Caledonia Presbyterian.

It was a misunderstanding.

"I can explain—"

"It's too late." Mom put her hands over her face again. "I already left. I told them I was tired of their gossip."

It took a long, horrific moment for her words to register. When they did, I wanted to die.

Mom quit. For me.

And there was only one person who knew about those stones.

Eugene.

CHAPTER FIFTEEN

MOM was still at the table when Dad got home. I lay on my bed, my door open. His footsteps stopped right inside the front door. Maybe he was startled that Mom was actually around.

"I don't have a job anymore," Mom said quietly.

The temperature in our house plummeted with those words.

"What?"

"I was fired." Mom paused. "Not really. I quit."

"You what?"

"I told Mr. Robinson that I didn't want to work for him anymore."

"Oh, my God. Rose, I knew there were problems, but why?"

"It's about Jewel."

"What does Jewel have to do with this?"

"Go ahead. Ask her."

"But—"

"I said ask her."

Silence.

Tears burned my eyes. If I hadn't been friends with Eugene, none of this would have happened.

It was all my fault.

"Jewel!" Dad called out.

I trudged into the dining room. Dad had dropped his briefcase in the middle of the kitchen.

"Sit down," he said.

I sat down.

"What happened, Jewel?" His voice wavered, like he was either mad or scared. Or both.

I wanted to answer, I really did. I wanted to say that I go to the cliff, where the earth takes care of my worries and I can just be me. That I met a friend who wasn't really a friend and I made the mistake of trusting him, and now I have a massive black hole swirling in my chest. That I'm ruining everyone's life.

I wanted to say all that, every last word, but I didn't. Instead I looked at my hands. A tear slid down my cheek.

"Jewel is still going to the cliff," Mom said.

Dad's eyebrows shot up.

"And Mr. Robinson said they've seen a circle of stones at the cliff, and there are rumors that Jewel does strange things with those stones. He doesn't know what goes on there; it's just a little too different." Mom paused. "He was laughing, like it was a joke, but I knew what he meant. And I told him," Mom continued, "how dare he insinuate that my daughter is doing anything wrong, and that he was too much of a coward to stand up to the rumors in his own community."

"You told him that?"

Mom smiled weakly. "He got angry when I called him a coward. And I was on a roll and said that I don't want to work for a coward either. Then I left."

I sniffled. "I didn't do anything wrong."

"What you did wrong was disobey," Mom said, turning to me. An edge crept into her voice. "What matters is I lost my job because you didn't listen to us."

"A circle of stones?" Dad asked. His voice was funny.

I swallowed. How come I have to tell them everything when they keep all these secrets from me?

"Answer your father," Mom said.

The dilemma: Which is worse, opening your mouth only to burst into tears, or remaining silent and absorbing their blame?

"You see what she's turning into?" Mom said to Dad. Her voice was still quiet. Almost pleading. "You've demented our daughter with your superstitions." She propped her forehead in both hands.

"I can talk to Mr. Robinson," I pleaded.

Mom groaned.

"I'll tell him everything so he'll believe me," I insisted.

Dad's jaw clenched. His Adam's apple moved up and down.

A whimpering noise came from behind Mom's hands. "How will we pay our mortgage?"

Dad stalked out of the dining room.

"Maybe Mrs. Jameson needs help," I whispered. "In the bakery."

Mom hit her fist on the table. "Who will hire me when I've upset the mayor?" she shouted. Her knuckles were white.

Something inside me caved, and I burst into tears. "I'll tell them that I didn't do anything wrong. And you could get your job back—"

"People believe what they choose to believe. Arguing won't help." Mom swore under her breath.

"I'm sorry, Mom!" I howled. "I'm so, so sorry."

"'Sorry' isn't going to keep a roof over our heads!"

Dad's feet pounded back down the hall. He held a brown

paper bag in one of his hands. The screen door slammed as he left the house, his shoes stabbing against the gravel.

"Nigel, where are you going?"

My stomach dropped. Mom and I ran out of the house and followed him. Dad got in the Buick.

"Get in."

We did.

Dad threw the car into gear and swerved down the driveway. His hands gripped the steering wheel, hard. Then he veered onto the road.

I knew the route we were taking. Dad was headed to the cliff.

"Jewel is a smart girl," Dad said, punching the gas pedal. The car lurched forward. "If you would have let me teach her, she would have known to stay away from the cliff."

A rabbit leaped into the road. Dad swerved to miss it.

"Nigel!" Mom cried as her shoulder slammed into the car door.

"But you've kept Jewel ignorant," Dad continued, ignoring her. "If she doesn't have a good head on her shoulders, it's because of you. You've done nothing to protect her."

"Nothing?" Mom cried. "You believe in hocus-pocus. That's ludicrous."

Dad braked hard as he pulled to the side of the road. He

threw his door open and stomped to the footpath. We had to run to keep up with him all the way to the cliff, and when he saw the circle he stopped cold. A strange cry came from his throat.

"This is your fault!" he shouted, turning on Mom. "All these years I've tried to protect her."

"Me?" Mom put her face inches from his. "I've been trying to protect her too!"

"I mean from duppies."

"And I mean from you."

It was so strange to have my parents at the cliff. With my circle. So wrong. Even the angle of the sunlight was wrong. My parents were standing on the place where I buried my pebbles, trampling them down.

"Jewel," Dad said, "this place is crawling with duppies." Then, almost to no one, he cried out, "I'm not losing another child to this cliff."

"This place is not *crawling with duppies*," Mom retorted, grabbing his arm. "This is exactly the nonsense that I've been trying to keep from Jewel."

"And how well has that been working out?" Dad asked, waving at the circle of stones. "No matter how much you deny the reality of the spirit world, it's here, pressing on us from all directions."

"This is stupid."

"And the spirits are angry at our family. Because of you, Rose. You refuse to respect them—"

"The only thing I've ever wanted is for Jewel to become a levelheaded, practical girl," Mom retorted.

Dad snorted. "Think what you like. It's clear that Jewel coming out here is a sign. Something is teaching her since we have not." Dad walked right to my circle and picked up a stone.

My seventh-year stone. My breath caught.

Dad looked at us. "And a duppy is waiting to trick her, too, if we don't stop it."

Then he heaved my stone over the cliff.

"Nooo!" I cried, running at him. "No! Please! Anything, please—" I grabbed his arm, but he shook me off. Mom dashed at me, took my arms, and held me in a bear grasp while I watched Dad tear up my circle and throw my stones, one by one by one, into that empty space. Then he took out his paper bag and threw fistfuls of rice onto the ground, sprinkled holy water, and put a crucifix where the circle used to be.

I heard screaming echo off the boulder, under the cloudless sky, for a long, long time. I'm still not sure that was me.

I didn't speak on the way home, or that evening, or the next day. Not one word. In fact, I didn't want to talk again for the rest of my life. When something you love is taken from you, words are pointless. What's the use of words if they're empty or powerless or fake? Why not be silent until the very last minute of forever?

Over the next week, my parents were home more. Mom got on the phone and called around town to see if anyone needed any help, which of course they didn't. Dad came home straightaway from work on the nights he wasn't putting in extra hours. He bought a lot of milk for cereal. And more rice.

I stayed in my room.

Mom tried to talk to me, and Dad, too; they tried to explain that by throwing my rocks off the cliff, they were protecting me. It was for my own good. But that kind of talk made my lips fuse shut. How could they say they were protecting me when they slit me open and scooped everything out? My head hurt every time I thought of what they said that awful afternoon.

It's incredible how differently we see things. I mean, someone could say, this is the sky. And someone else could come along and say, oh no, this is the house of the spirits. And they'd be looking at the exact same thing. Or someone could say, this is a special place, and another person would say it's just a bunch of stones. And then a third person would say, actually this is a dangerous place and throw the stones over a cliff.

My throat got tight. I got up, took my rock collection off my shelf, and held as many as I could in my hands, gripping them hard until my fingers hurt. And even though I tried not to think about it, I kept seeing my stones fall into the emptiness.

But I didn't want to think about things falling anymore. So I put my rocks down on my bed and played with the golden chain around my neck, which was smooth beneath my fingers.

Suddenly, for the first time, I saw Bird jumping off and flying instead. It was an incredible sight, seeing my brother's arms outstretched again, embracing the sky, his face smiling like the sun. A shiver went down my back. Who knows, I thought, maybe Bird *did* fly that day, and now my big brother is out there, soaring.

A fat, black fly stopped droning about my room and perched on the back of my desk chair. It stood there, still, for a long time, staring at me. Then it rubbed its hind legs over its wings and abdomen, over and over and over, taking out the dust and dirt, then cleaning the underside of its wings, shivering those wings, which were glowing spiderwebs.

There was a light tap on my door. I went over and opened it a peek. A thin slice of Grandpa appeared in front of me.

He'd never knocked on my door before. I opened it wider and gave him a look that said, *My words still don't want to come out.*

The edges of his lips curved up slightly, and I felt better when he did that. If there was anyone who would understand about not talking, it was Grandpa.

His eyes flicked around my room. I pulled out my chair and there we sat, him in the chair and me on my bed, the both of us silent. I felt stupid, like I should be saying or doing something, and I made to get up and maybe bring out my dominoes, even though I really didn't want to. But Grandpa put his hand up, like, *It's okay to just sit and do nothing.* So I sat back down, confused. After a while, something changed and the strangeness left the room, and it was actually nice, being quiet together.

I had never shared silence with someone before. In my house we wield silence like shields and swords: We use it to push people away or injure them. But there Grandpa and I were, sitting in my room, and it was totally different. Instead, the quiet that fell over us was the softest, safest blanket you could ever imagine. A blanket where I could just be me.

Grandpa must have known what happened with Mom and Dad and me and the cliff—either because of all the shouting or all the silence. But this time, though Grandpa and I didn't say a single word, I could still make out his message, loud and clear: *I'm still here.*

We sat like that for a long time in that warm and comforting room, our hearts hanging wide open. I learned then that hearts don't speak with words like how we think they do in movies or in songs; I think they need a lot more space than that. Anyway, all I really knew was that my heart had an awful, raging fever that day, and in the silence, Grandpa brought with him the cooling rain.

CHAPTER SIXTEEN

I SNUCK out a couple nights later and went to McLaren's tree. I couldn't help it. I missed my cliff—it was like I was missing an arm or a leg—and I figured that a tree in the middle of a field couldn't be all that bad. Dad didn't say there were any duppies around those parts. To tell the truth, though, I was sick of hearing my parents say they were doing things *for my own good,* when really I was getting suspicious that they didn't know very much at all.

Anyone could hear him approach from miles away, he was so loud.

"You up there?"

Just hearing Eugene's voice made me tense up.

I looked down. "Yup. And I don't want to hear anything

about how I'm not supposed to be in this tree because you were never, ever supposed to tell and I'm never going to talk to you again, *Eugene*." And just as soon as those words tumbled out of my mouth, I realized I was speaking again, and I was speaking to him, which I just said I wouldn't do.

"I'm really sorry about my name."

"I'm not talking about your stupid name. I'm talking about the cliff."

"What?"

"You know what I'm talking about," I said, peering down at him. I half wanted to run down and give him a huge hug because I missed him and half wanted to take one of those tree limbs on his hill and give him a good whack.

Eugene scratched the back of his neck. "What about the cliff?"

He was doing a good job at faking it, that was for sure. But he wasn't going to fool me again. "Stop it. And now my mom doesn't have a job because of you and they're blaming me and we might be kicked out of our house, so thanks for nothing."

"Jewel, I don't know what you're talking about. I didn't say anything."

"Who did you tell?" I demanded. But I was starting to get confused inside.

"About the cliff? No one," he said simply. "But your mom lost her job?"

I was so stirred up I didn't trust myself to speak, and in that pause Eugene climbed up the rope. He sat on the second branch, the one right below mine.

"Either tell me or get back down," I said. I was surprised at how bossy I sounded.

"Is your mom okay?" Eugene asked.

"Just tell me who you told," I said loudly. "And then go and tell everyone that it was another of your big, fat lies."

Eugene didn't say anything for a long time, and the crickets whirred through the night, shivering the air around us. I thought he was going to slip back down the tree and head home, but instead he said, "Jewel."

"What?" I said, agitated.

"I've been coming out here every night since . . . you know," he said. His voice was tentative. "So I could apologize to you about my name."

A lump suddenly formed in my throat. "Really?" I asked. "Is that the truth?" My voice caught.

"Sure is. I would stand at the base of the trunk and say, 'You up there?' and if you weren't, I'd head back home. I have the mosquito bites to prove it."

A dam that I didn't know was in me burst open, and I

pressed the heels of my hands to my eyes to stop the tears, but it didn't help. "How can you apologize about your name but not about the cliff?" I asked. "Don't you know what you did to us?"

"Jewel," Eugene said quietly, "I didn't say anything about the cliff."

"But they *know*," I insisted.

"Who?"

"Mr. Robinson, everyone." Tears flowed off my chin. "People are talking about me spending so much time at the cliff, with my stones," I said, "and Mr. Robinson didn't want one of his employees to be the cause of so much talk."

"Are you serious?"

"So Mom told him she didn't want to work for someone who didn't have the courage to stand up to gossip, and left."

"She did that?" Eugene sounded impressed.

That upset me even more. "She doesn't have a job because of you!" I said.

"But I didn't say anything about your cliff," he insisted. "Not a word."

"How can I trust you, John?" I cried.

He shifted on his branch.

"I mean Eugene," I said quietly.

"No, it's okay," he said. "Look, Jewel." He took a deep

breath. "I said I was John as a joke, at first. I didn't know you at all; you were just the girl in the weird family whose kid brother died and there was this strange talk about curses and spirits. I knew you were the Campbell girl the moment you came walking to this tree."

"You knew it was me from the road?" I asked, confused.

"Who else would be walking from the direction of your house, looking like no one around here?" he asked.

"Oh."

"So I said my name was John." He paused. "To freak you out a little, maybe, okay. Because my uncle said your family is superstitious. But I didn't think you'd be so smart or fun. And the longer I was John, the better it felt. The better *I* felt."

"But how did your uncle know about . . . your name?" I asked.

"When my uncle first told me about you guys, I laughed and said, 'Wouldn't it be great if I pretended my name was John?' and my uncle said, 'Don't you dare,' and I told him I was just talking. Nothing serious. He had no idea what was going on until you came over that night and asked for John.

"And anyway," he continued, "what's the big deal lying about a name?"

I looked at him, confused. That seemed pretty big to me.

"I lie all the time to my parents—in fact, they like it when I lie to them."

"That's not true," I said.

"Yes, it is," Eugene replied.

I didn't know what to say to that. He sounded so certain—but how could that be, his parents like it when he lies? The lightning bugs were coming out, little lights scattered all over the earth. Lights above, lights below.

"Are you really adopted?" I asked.

Eugene paused. "Yes."

"And your real name is Eugene."

Another pause. "Yes."

"And Mr. McLaren is really your uncle," I said.

"Yes," Eugene said. "I'm visiting him because Mom is having a baby. Of her own." His voice got tight. "And my parents dumped me off at my uncle's house while they got the nursery ready."

My stomach sank. No wonder he didn't want to talk about his uncle. Or his family. How could they do that to him?

"And everyone wants me to say that I'm happy about the baby. So I do. Even though it's all a lie. And the more I say it, the more they like it, even though they know it's a lie too." Eugene stopped for a while and watched the lightning bugs. "That seems like a lot worse than just lying about a name."

A slight breeze blew, and it quivered the leaves like rain. "I don't know what happened about the cliff," Eugene said. "But I want to help."

I thought for a long, hard moment. "Okay," I said finally. When I said that, his moon-teeth smile opened up, and I got all shiny inside.

We climbed down from the tree, and when we reached the bottom, Eugene said, "You can still call me John if you want."

"No, that's okay," I said slowly. "But you won't get mad at me if 'John' slips out every once in a while, will you?"

"Only if you don't get mad at me for never eating Reservation Chicken again," he said.

I instantly remembered the look on his face at the dinner table. He'd never have to worry about eating Mom's cooking, but I could tell him about that later. So I laughed hard instead and felt lighter, like I could breathe again. Like I was coming home.

The next day when I looked out my window, I was startled to see that Dad's tree saplings weren't doing so well. In fact, they were drooped down and withered. With all the hours Dad had been putting in at Max's Appliances to make more money for us, he hadn't had time to take care of his garden.

What was worse, the rosemary was dried-up, dead. Every last bit of it.

No one seemed to notice that besides me. I even caught Grandpa taking the red sweater and socks and the horseshoe down off the wall, as if no one needed the extra layers of protection anymore.

My parents didn't notice much of anything because they were too busy acting strange, as if I was going to break at any minute, like I wasn't a jewel, all tough from being in the ground for hundreds of thousands of years. Instead, they talked quietly and made sure not to look at me more than usual. I wished I could be who they wanted me to be, the good kid who didn't give them any problems, but it was too late for that.

I bit my lip. I couldn't do much, but at least I could water what remained of Dad's garden. I lugged the hose across our backyard and made little pools of water around each sapling, then around the tomatoes and cucumbers. Then I pulled up the dead rosemary, all the way down to the roots, and threw it in the garbage. Grandpa must have been watching me from his window because he came out there and stood with me under the cloudy sky.

I was thinking about the rosemary I'd just torn out, and

how I felt kind of ripped up, and how Grandpa must feel that way sometimes when he wants to use words to speak and can't. We were quiet for a while when I turned to him and said, "Grandpa, why don't you talk?"

He jolted a little bit, startled. Like I asked a question I wasn't supposed to ask. Or maybe it was because I was talking again.

"Your tapes were fantastic." I gave a little smile. "I really liked the part where you were at the river, splashing and yelling up a storm." Mom had pulled up some river weed from the mucked-up bottom and put some down Dad's pants. Dad screamed like a lunatic. So did Mom, but in the victorious way.

I moved the hose to the next plants. It was good I was watering the garden; I didn't have to look at him. "And I loved how you and Granny were always joking around, telling stories about each other."

Out of the corner of my eye, I caught Grandpa sucking in his breath.

"And I know that Bird dying was really sad and all, but why don't you talk?" I lifted my eyes to his, finally. "What happened that night?"

Grandpa's lips twitched, and a sadness covered him, as if he were suddenly back at the pond.

"You can tell me, Grandpa," I said. "I won't say anything—"

He tensed, and I followed his eyes. Mom was coming down the sloping grass to where we were. "Jewel, I've been looking everywhere for you," she said, but her eyes bugged out at Grandpa and me together.

"We've been here this whole time," I said.

Her head jerked back. This was the first time I'd spoken in days. "That's so great, honey," she said, all happy. Then she realized that she wasn't making sense. "I mean, I'm glad you're feeling better."

I shrugged. "A little."

"Well, that's terrific." She glanced at Grandpa again. "I'd like for you to get ready. We have an appointment to go to."

I gave her a look. "We do?"

"Well, you and me," she said quickly. Why was she acting like Grandpa wasn't standing next to me? She hadn't even acknowledged him. "And we need to get going if we're going to be on time."

"Okay." I turned to Grandpa. "Could you finish watering the garden?"

Grandpa took the hose.

"Thanks," I said.

Mom's jaw dropped. Then she blushed.

It served her right, being so rude like that.

The appointment happened to be with a priest in a church forty miles away—far enough so no one would know about us.

"But why?" I asked as we pulled onto the highway. "We don't go to church anymore."

"I know, honey," Mom said. "But Dad and I thought it best that you . . . talk with someone."

"About what?"

"There have to be other people," she continued, ignoring my question, "but he wanted to try this first."

I sighed. Rain streaked against my window. It came down pretty steady, and it turned the land soft and gray. I suppose we didn't need to water the garden, I thought, picking at the peeling vinyl on the side of the door. Even though it had been nice to spend some time with Grandpa.

But Grandpa would be really upset if he found out that I was friends with Eugene again. I got scrunched up inside thinking about yet another secret. But seriously, if Grandpa found out I was talking with Eugene, he'd run and get a fresh bushel of rosemary, straightaway.

Somehow I just kept messing things up.

"Jewel, don't pick at the door," Mom said as she pulled into the parking lot of a church. A sign in front said ST. MICHAEL'S PARISH WELCOMES YOU!

"Can I help you?" asked the receptionist as we stepped inside. She had poufy blond hair that couldn't be a real color. I mean, hair like that doesn't just happen to people.

She stared at my hair. Maybe she was thinking the same thing.

"We have an appointment with Father Jim," Mom said.

"Ah, yes," she said, her eyes going back and forth between Mom and me, as if trying to figure out how we're related. Then she smiled. "Let me get him."

She led us into a little room with a cross and a lot of books and some comfy chairs. After a little while a man stepped in and shook our hands. "Good to meet you, Mrs. Campbell," he said. His nose had a bump on it, like a tiny turtle had dug under his skin, but his smile reached all the way into his eyes.

"This is my daughter, Jewel," Mom said. "And we're here because she has . . . a problem."

"What kind of problem?" Father Jim asked, settling back into his chair. He looked at me expectantly.

This was what they wanted? For me to tell some stranger that I have problems with duppies and circles and rocks? My chest burned with anger, and I gripped the sides of my chair, hard.

"We all have problems in our lives," Father Jim said, his voice calm and nice. "Sometimes it's good to talk about it."

We'll see about that, I thought.

"Jewel, tell the priest about what happened," Mom said, her voice sharpening.

I sat for a moment, trying to figure out what Mom wanted me to say. Then it hit me. I was sick of trying to make Mom happy. Dad too. They're not trying to make *me* happy, I thought. They threw my stones over the cliff and forbade me from going there again. They treat Grandpa like an idiot. They don't want me to dig for arrowheads or talk about anything important or do anything that makes me truly, truly happy.

I looked straight at Father Jim. "There are a lot of problems," I said.

He waited.

"Like, Mom doesn't make us go to church anymore because she says religion is a bunch of lies to keep people obedient."

"Jewel!" Mom cried.

"But I think there are a lot of things out there that we don't know about, and they're out there and they sure know about us."

Mom stood up and grabbed my arm. "We are going," she snapped.

Father Jim raised a hand. "Mrs. Campbell, don't you think it's worthwhile to hear your daughter's perspective?"

I didn't wait for Mom to answer. "And Dad is a Christian too, but he believes in other things, like duppies and bad luck and good luck, even though he doesn't talk about it in front of others because in this country people would say he's superstitious," I said.

"Please, Mrs. Campbell," Father Jim said, gesturing to Mom's chair.

Mom's face got dark. She sat back down.

"And my parents are really mad at me because I go to the cliff where my brother tried to fly."

"Tried to fly?"

Mom put her head in her hands.

"Yeah," I said, "but instead he fell and died. He was five."

Silence.

Father Jim's eyebrows lifted. "I'm so sorry about your brother, Jewel," he said, and he meant it. "That's tragic."

I shrugged, but my throat got tight.

Father Jim crossed his legs. "And you go to this cliff? What kinds of things do you do there?"

"I talk to my rocks—or I used to," I said, shooting a murderous look at Mom.

Mom exhaled loudly.

"Rocks." Father Jim peered at me intently.

"Well, and to the grasses and the sky and the sun. They talk to me." I was on a roll now. And Father Jim looked really interested, which made me want to keep going. "The cliff is special," I said. "There's something there."

"Like what?"

I shrugged. "I don't know. But the moment you go there, you know it's different—it doesn't feel like how a gas station or a grocery store feels." I shifted in my chair. "It's . . . special. Like how the inside of a church is special."

Father Jim leaned forward. "What do your rocks say?"

I thought about that for a bit. They don't use words, exactly, but I can hear them anyway. Like Grandpa. It's a different kind of talking, a different kind of listening. "They say something like, 'We care about you,'" I said.

The grandfather clock in the room ticked loudly, and each swing of the pendulum measured out the seconds that no one spoke. I really wanted to tell Father Jim about how I bury my pebbles too, but Mom was jiggling the foot that was crossed over her leg, which meant nothing good.

Father Jim finally turned to Mom. "When was the last time you came to mass?" he asked gently.

Mom's lips pursed, like she would bolt out of there if it wasn't for me. "Five years," she said. "Maybe six."

"And you're worried about your daughter's experiences at the cliff," Father Jim said.

"Her father and I both are, for different reasons."

Father Jim stood up and crossed over to his shelf of books. "There are a lot of ways that God talks to us," he said. "Many times, it's through the church. But if Jewel hasn't been raised in the church, then God will talk to his children in other ways."

Mom sat stiller than a statue.

Father Jim pulled out a book. "There was a great man who talked to stones too," he said to me.

"Really?" I asked. This time I was the one leaning forward.

"He talked to the sun and the moon and, well, everything."

"Where does he live?" I asked.

Father Jim chuckled. "He's been dead for a good couple centuries. His name is Saint Francis."

"Excuse me," Mom said sharply. "My daughter put a circle of stones at the cliff. I have lost my job over this."

Father Jim's shoulders straightened.

"My husband thinks evil spirits are there. I'm not going to sit in this room and hear you tell my daughter she's a saint because she talks to rocks." Mom leaned over and grabbed her purse.

"Saint Francis endured much pain and poverty," Father Jim said.

I nodded my head vigorously. "We can't pay our bills."

A small sound came from Mom's throat. "Enough. We're going."

But I didn't move. "Father Jim, do evil spirits exist? Do duppies trick us?"

Mom froze. Father Jim sat there awhile and rubbed the underside of his chin. Finally he said, "There are spirits out there, angels and demons, good ones and bad ones. We need to be vigilant about what kind they are and what kind we trust."

"How do we know what kind they are?" I pressed.

"It can be hard to discern because they come in many different forms," Father Jim said. "The best way is to notice what they want us to do. Are they asking us to glorify God? Or ourselves?"

I wasn't sure if talking to my rocks was glorifying anything, but they always felt like home to me.

"Sometimes God talks to us through humans," Father Jim continued, "but he can use all of creation."

"Because God is everywhere," I said.

"Yes."

"So my rocks are beautiful because I'm seeing a part of God."

Father Jim smiled. Then, because Mom really wanted to

leave at that point, he said a quick prayer, that God would protect us from evil and that we could find God's blessings all around us. He also thanked God for remembering to make stones, because stones can teach us how to endure.

I liked that.

CHAPTER SEVENTEEN

MOM didn't say anything on the way home, which was fine with me. That gave me time to think about what Father Jim had said. And the more I thought about it, the more questions I had. Do angels and saints have to be human? If not, then Mr. McLaren's tree had to be an angel, the way it brought Eugene and me back together.

But angels and saints felt a long ways away as Mom pulled into our driveway. The sun hung above the trees.

"Well?" Dad asked, coming out to meet us. The angle of the sun made a golden outline around him. He wiped his hands on his pants. They were covered with flour.

"It was a splendid time," Mom said dryly. "The priest says that saints talk to rocks too, so there's nothing to be worried about."

"He said that?" Dad shifted, and with him, the light.

Mom smirked. "In fact, he and Jewel got along quite well."

"Did he pray over her?"

"He said a prayer."

"No," Dad said, his forehead wrinkling up. "I meant—"

"Did he exorcise the demons?" Mom asked. She readjusted the purse on her shoulder. "No, Nigel, he did not. I guess he didn't see the need. Maybe next time, before I do you a favor, we should talk about exactly what you want me to demand of a priest."

I left them to argue in the driveway, blinking back tears. I wasn't sure which was worse, slicing into someone with silence or with words.

I knocked on Grandpa's door. When there wasn't any answer, I peeked inside. He wasn't there. Back in my room, I slipped in one of Grandpa's mento tapes, but even his music couldn't lift the weight off my chest, not with Dad and Mom's comments seeping into our walls. So I went into the kitchen and put on my shoes again.

"Where are you going?" Dad asked. He looked directly at me, like I was a thief.

"Out," I said.

"Don't talk to your dad with that tone of voice," Mom said.

"I'm not going to the cliff," I said. And before they could get on my back about *that* tone of voice, I left the house.

It was just as I thought: There were footprints through the grasses on the deer path. I followed the trail around until it opened up and revealed the pond. And Grandpa. He was sitting exactly where he had been before, his head in his hands, his back deeply curved. The pond was a soft pastel, almost a mirror to the sky.

I cupped my hands to my mouth. "Hey, Grandpa," I called.

Grandpa's head lifted, and he looked at me for a long while, like a deer that doesn't know if it should stay or flee. I waved a little. He raised his hand awkwardly, and I walked down the grassy slope to where he was. He scooted over so I could sit next to him.

The cicadas were loud. It was beautiful and haunting at the same time. How could something so small make so much noise? Or someone as large as Grandpa make no sound at all?

But an entire universe full of silence was still better than how Dad and Mom were now talking to each other, each word awful and cold. Where was the laughter and happiness from that Valentine's Day on the tape? Joy is like a child, I realized, as I picked at the bark by my thigh. You feed it or it dies.

"Grandpa," I said, "why are my parents so angry all the time?"

I knew better than to ask him something other than a yes-or-no question, but I couldn't help myself.

Grandpa exhaled through his nose and shook his head. I didn't quite know what he meant by that.

"And why are you so sad?" I asked.

He turned to me. I never realized how deep and full and dark his eyes were until that very moment. They were soft and endless, in an awful way, like those black holes that go on and on, never stopping for forever. I wanted to cry just looking at Grandpa. Maybe that's why he made sure never to look at anyone.

"You made so many tapes," I said, a little shaken. "I like the way you laughed."

Grandpa's face grew even longer, and he turned toward the pond. Then he stood up, and after a while I did too, and we watched the pond grow pink and orange and purple, until it looked like it was on fire. I was sure then that this pond knew Grandpa as well as my cliff knew me. As I was marveling at how the earth holds our sadness in many kinds of ways, Grandpa put his arm around my shoulder. Then it was my turn to turn into a deer, startled and not knowing what to do; his arm was warm and awkward and gentle, though, and my heart was beating a million times a minute because *this was Pooba*.

"It's all about Bird, isn't it?" I said, and it wasn't really a question.

Grandpa kept looking away from me in a way that said yes.

"You mean he's actually *nice*?" Eugene asked later that night. We were at Event Horizon. Eugene clicked his flashlight on and off, on and off, like he was a big lightning bug.

"Grandpa's more than nice. He shares his music with me," I said. Eugene and I had a lot of catching up to do.

"Well, I'll be dipped." The light went out. Then on. "So what happened?" Eugene asked. "Why the change?"

Light out.

I shrugged. "Don't know. But it's really different now."

Light on.

"Huh. So does that mean he won't punch me in the face anymore?"

Light out.

"Oh, you mean like this?" I asked, and in the blackness I reached out and squeezed his face.

"Hey, stop that!" he shouted, but he was laughing.

I was laughing too, and snatched the flashlight from his

hands. "Stop turning the stupid flashlight on and off," I replied, and I clicked the light on and threw it at him.

We grew quiet after a while. A starry-night kind of quiet. It felt like I hadn't been to Event Horizon for a million years, and considering that the last time I was here it was with *John*, I suppose I was right. We looked up through the tree and into the circle of stars above us. There are some pretty good things about being an astronaut. You could see the stars up close. You could leave your problems behind.

"Actually, I think Grandpa would still punch you in the face," I said.

Eugene's head jerked back a little. "Why?" he asked.

"Because," I said, feeling like the teacher this time, "Grandpa probably still thinks you're a duppy."

Eugene snorted. "I'm a duppy?"

I forgot I never told him that. "Your name was John, you look a little close to what Bird might have looked like, and Grandpa thought you were a duppy in a human form, tricking me. So he punched you."

"Wow." Eugene shook his head.

"Well, you *were* tricking me," I pointed out. "Just not how Grandpa thought."

"A duppy taking a human form?" Eugene asked. He rolled

his eyes. "Please." Eugene grabbed a granola bar from his stash. "I'll tell him I'm not a duppy."

"Doesn't matter," I said. "That's what he thinks." Eugene gave a bar to me, and I took a hungry bite. You could really get addicted to these things. "Same thing with Mr. Robinson," I continued. "Even Mom doesn't think she can get him to understand."

"Then it looks like we'll have to talk to him ourselves," Eugene said.

I tried to figure out if he was kidding or not.

"I'm serious. Let's go tomorrow," he said as he shoved the whole granola bar in his mouth. It turned into a big wad of goo. He couldn't even close his mouth, it was so big.

I laughed. Eugene tried to laugh too but couldn't, which made me laugh harder. "Looking like that, Grandpa would *definitely* punch you in the face," I said.

Eugene elbowed me. He chewed on his granola for a long time, making smacking noises. Finally he said, "Why's your grandpa so angry?"

"I asked him why he was sad," I said. "It's because of Bird."

"Right. But why is he *angry*?"

That stumped me. Growing up, I never questioned why Grandpa was angry. He just was. That was how things were. The sun rises. The sun sets. The moon comes out. Grandpa's angry. But I guess that someone could have different layers, like the earth, different strata piled one on top of the other. If you dig you can hit another layer inside someone. And sometimes those layers are surprising.

"Well," I said, "he did kill Bird. By accident." The tips of my fingers made little circles on the earthen floor. I tried to push down something mad and bubbly in my stomach when I thought about how this came back to Bird. Again. "It's just . . . my brother's been dead my whole life, but everyone's still fighting about him. Like he's right in our house."

"Maybe he is," Eugene said.

"Something happened that day," I insisted. "Grandpa told me so."

"How'd he tell you if he can't talk?"

I picked at a mosquito bite on my leg. "You can say tons of things without talking."

We got quiet then, as if talking about not talking made our mouths all shy. We ducked out of Event Horizon and walked to the edge of the trees, where the sprawled-out stars stretched from one horizon to the other. Then, through the crickets and the breeze that was blowing over the dark rows of corn, there was that silence again, a silence warm and thick and comforting like a blanket. I'd give anything in the whole wide world, I realized, to be surrounded by people and rocks and plants that could wrap me in that silence.

Eugene spoke then, but softly, as if he could feel it too. "You know," he said, "you and your brother are like a close binary system."

"A what?"

"A close binary system. Stars, you know. Stars are rarely ever alone." His voice got funny. "Stars can come in clusters, but they most frequently come in pairs. A binary system."

"Oh." It was nice to think of Bird and me like that, twinkling pretty in the sky.

"Sometimes stars in binary systems orbit each other really closely, much closer than normal. That's why they're called *close* binary systems. And the star with less mass orbits its companion, which has more mass."

"And more gravity," I pointed out.

Eugene grinned. "Sometimes these two stars orbit so closely that they transfer matter to each other."

"They what?"

"Parts of them fly off and get pulled in by the gravitational pull of the companion star. And vice versa. Each star is changed by the other."

"They each have parts of the other?" I asked.

"Yup," Eugene said. "And because of that, the stars'

compositions change, as well as how they develop in the future." He craned his neck up to the sky. "It's like with you and Bird. He's in you. And you are in him, wherever he is."

I don't know why, but I started to cry right then, the second time that I cried in front of Eugene in just a couple days. I don't like crying in front of people because it shows them the holes that you have on the inside. I guess with all the crying I'd been doing lately, I had more holes than I thought. It was okay with Eugene, though. He stood next to me, close, not touching, but in the way he stood, all attentive, his heart must have been talking to mine, and mine must have been listening, because after a while I felt better. When I caught my breath, Eugene started pointing out the constellations, one by one.

And, he reminded me, the Perseids were coming soon.

CHAPTER EIGHTEEN

IT turned out that Eugene was completely serious about talking to Mr. Robinson. The next day, we met up on our bikes in front of our town hall.

"We're crazy," I said to Eugene. He was even wearing a nice shirt for the occasion.

"Who else is going to do it?" He grinned.

We stepped inside the cool office just in time to see Mrs. Bowers, the secretary, finish putting on mascara. That was pretty funny since she's old, and it's pointless for old people to put on mascara. In Caledonia there's no one to notice it, anyway.

"Why, Jewel," she said, giving a fake smile. "What brings you here?" Then her eyes got round when she saw Eugene.

"And with your friend. What's your name again? You're Tim's nephew, right?"

"I'm Eugene," he said, nice and polite.

"Ah, yes. Eugene." She picked up a pen and twiddled it between her fingers. "Tim's told me about you."

Eugene smiled.

Mrs. Bowers was talking really loud. It was the kind of loud that people talk when they're uncomfortable or scared. I glanced around in the waiting area. Mrs. Jameson was there, her long hair pulled into a ponytail at her neck. She flipped through a magazine.

"I'd like to talk to Mr. Robinson," I said, trying to sound grown-up.

"Oh, dear," Mrs. Bowers said, not looking very upset at all, "I'm afraid you'll need to set up an appointment for that."

"An appointment?" I asked. "But these are his open hours." Mr. Robinson had long ago announced his open hours, when anyone in the community could talk to him about their concerns. Mom said it was an excuse for a gossip fest, but I thought it sounded rather practical.

"These are his open hours," Mrs. Bowers said. She didn't look at me. "But he's quite busy right now."

"We can wait," I said.

"I'm afraid you'll need to make an appointment."

Boy, was my blood starting to boil. I took a deep breath. "But why would I—"

"Is this because of Jewel's mom?" Eugene cut in. "Because it shouldn't matter what Jewel wants to talk about if these are the open hours."

Mrs. Bowers sucked in a breath. "Oh, it's not that," she said, her voice getting higher. "It's just . . . he usually doesn't talk to children."

"That's too bad for his kids," I said.

"Now that's enough," Mrs. Bowers snapped. Her eyes narrowed. "I'm not sure why you two are here—"

"We're here," I said, just as loudly as her this time, "to tell Mr. Robinson that he's a coward for being afraid of people's talk, and that those stones at the cliff have nothing to do with him and are none of his business."

Mrs. Bowers's jaw hit the desk.

"And now my mom doesn't have a job and she's really sad," I said. "Even though Mr. Robinson is the mayor and all, that doesn't mean he should be believing everything he hears. And sometimes he should stand up for people, like my mom. And," I added, because I was on a roll and couldn't stop if I tried, "since that's what I was going to tell him, I guess I don't need to see him during his gossip fest after all. Please give him the message."

Mrs. Bowers smiled coldly. "No problem, Jewel. I will."

I didn't move, though, and neither did Eugene.

"Is there something else?" Mrs. Bowers snapped. "I'm rather busy."

"We're waiting for you to write the message," Eugene said.

Mrs. Bowers turned as pink as an eraser, and she snatched a pad of paper and scribbled something down.

As we turned to leave, I saw Mrs. Jameson quickly averting her eyes from us. But then she looked back at me, and in that sliver of an instant I could tell she had already heard about Mom.

Everyone had.

"Let's go to the cliff," I said to Eugene when we burst outside.

"Are you sure?" he asked.

I spun around and stuck my face right in his. "I'm going," I said. "You can come if you want."

He put his hands up. "Okay, okay." But he was smiling.

"I'm not going to have anyone tell me where I can't go and make up things that they don't know anything about and that's not even true," I said, my mouth going so fast I wasn't sure if I was making sense. I don't think I'd ever done that before, just shoot off at the mouth, but it sure felt great. Eugene's eyebrows were practically hanging at the top of his forehead, he was so surprised. I mean, I'd filled him in on what had happened, but I guess it didn't hit him how different everything was until I was right up in his face.

We rode our bikes through the two blocks of Broad Street that was our downtown and took the shortest way to get to the cliff. It felt great to have Eugene back. I mean, Grandpa's terrific and all, but I know for a fact that Grandpa would not have stood there in front of Mrs. Bowers and let me talk all snotty to her.

I could have gone to the cliff with my eyes closed, like there was this invisible string attached to my heart, stretched taut, pulling me across the road and fields, right to the cliff. It was right then that I realized that places in many ways are like people: They think about you when you're gone, wait for you to come back, and rejoice when you do. Eugene and I dumped our bikes in a ditch, and I ran on the path, not fast, but not too slow either, my fingers spread wide, ready to catch everything that I missed. Eugene kept up with me, not complaining, not even asking why, like he already knew.

We were almost there when I started laughing.

"What is it?" Eugene asked. He was breathing hard.

"When you said, 'We're waiting for you to write the

message'—that's exactly what *I* was going to say."

"You're kidding." Eugene threw me a huge smile.

I shook my head. "There was no way I was leaving until I saw Mrs. Bowers write that stupid note."

"Neither was I!" Eugene cried. "Wouldn't it have been funny if we said it at the same time?"

"We could have told her we just put a spell on her by doing that. She would have poked herself in the eye with her mascara, she'd have been so scared," I said. I was smiling, big-time.

When we came to the cliff, though, I stopped cold.

"Wow," Eugene said, stunned.

I guess there was a part of me that just didn't want it to be true, that Dad threw my rocks over the cliff. And there was a big chunk of me that was hoping those rocks jumped back up through the air while I was gone, soared up above the jagged ravine walls and plopped back down to where they'd been.

I kept staring. My circle really was gone. The crucifix already had a light layer of dirt over it.

My parents threw my circle away.

When something bad happens, sometimes it's so awful there aren't any words to describe it. And when something really, *really* bad happens, you go numb inside because even your heart doesn't know what to do. Like, it's feeling lots of sadness and terrible things one moment, and then—poof!—it just shuts down.

Maybe hearts can die like that.

"I can't believe your parents did this," Eugene said.

"It was to protect me," I replied bitterly. I glanced around. The area where I buried my pebbles was disturbed and pressed down from when Mom and Dad trampled them. Twelve dark marks sat in a circle on the earth, like ghosts.

I grabbed the crucifix and chucked it as hard as I could over the cliff. It spiraled a little as it arched through the air, before gravity took over, before it plummeted. I couldn't see where it actually landed. And it didn't matter anymore, I realized. The numbness inside grew bigger: A moment ago, it sat somewhere left of my spleen. Now the numbness spread through my lungs and stomach and kidneys, hollowing me out from the inside.

Nothing matters, I realized. Only Bird matters. And he flew away.

"I can't stand them," I said slowly.

Eugene leaned closer. "What?"

"I can't stand them," I said louder. Harsher. "My parents." I bent down and put my hand on the earth where my seventh-year rock used to be. "They just think about Bird," I said, brushing my fingertips over the silken dirt. "They fight about Bird. They're sad about Bird." My hands clenched into fists. "What about me?"

"Jewel—"

"What about me?" I repeated. It felt so good to say that, so freeing, like there was a key inside my chest and those words just unlocked something that had been pressed down inside, pent-up, forgotten. "Do you know they never asked me why I come here?" I asked, and the anger inside me gushed from that locked-up space. "Do you know they don't even look at me? Not really—not like how you or Grandpa look at me."

Eugene's eyebrows knitted together. "Right now I'm looking at you because I've never seen you like this."

"And I don't care about duppies or not-duppies anymore. What they fight about is stupid, anyway." I sized up the boulder. "You know, I've never climbed to the top. Let's do it. Now."

Eugene grabbed my shoulders. "Come on. Let's get out of here, Jewel."

"But what if Bird didn't fall?" I insisted.

"What do you mean?" Eugene's voice grew more agitated.

"What if he jumped and flew?"

"You're stupid for talking like this. Of course he fell."

"What if people really don't fall if they jump off the cliff?

What would you do if you saw me fly? If I actually tried it?"

"Do you want me to hit you?" he shouted into my face. "Is that what it'll take to get you to shut up?"

I pushed his arms back. "Oh, so you're the only one who can fly away, Mr. Astronaut? Mr. I'm-going-to-leave-everyone-behind-even-my-friends?"

Eugene stood there, stunned. I didn't realize I was shouting until I heard my anger echoing in the air. "That's not what I meant," Eugene said. "You know that."

I turned away. The grasses were tall now, August tall. I took a couple steps from Eugene, grabbed one of the long grasses, and ran my hand along its stem, bunching the seeds at my fingertips.

Eugene shoved his hands in his pockets, stalked over to the boulder, and kicked it a couple times. Then he leaned his forehead against the granite rock and closed his eyes. I was confused; I thought he wanted to leave.

"You know what I hate?" Eugene said quietly.

I grabbed another length of grass and bunched up the seeds. I waited.

"I hate the question 'Do you have siblings?'" He laughed, but he wasn't really laughing. "I can never answer that question. Not really." Something changed in his voice, and I could tell he wasn't really talking to me.

"Because who knows," he went on. "Maybe my birth mom did have other kids. My brothers and sisters. Maybe she decided to keep those kids." He tilted his head against the boulder. "Maybe not."

My stomach did little somersaults just then. He was right. I mean, even though my answer was, *I had a brother once and he died a long time ago,* at least I had an answer.

"Sometimes it gets to be too much, all the questions," Eugene was saying. "Sometimes I just want to leave it behind. Everything."

"But people care about you," I said.

"My parents care more about their new kid," Eugene said darkly. Then, after a split second he got it. He held my gaze for a long time, until his eyes wavered and he had to look away.

I plucked a third blade of grass. "You know, the boulder understands how you feel."

Eugene's lips twisted up. "Really?" he said, a little mockingly.

"Sure. It's an erratic."

He peered at me. "What do you mean?"

"Iowa doesn't have granite," I said. "We have sandstone and limestone and dolomites. Sedimentary rocks. Granites are north of here—Canada, even. But the boulder sitting right here is granite." I nodded. "Straight fact."

"So how did it get here?" Eugene asked.

"Glacial movements," I responded. "During the last ice age, glaciers picked up rocks and all kinds of things from one area and plunked them down in another, sometimes even a thousand miles away."

"Really?" Eugene's voice was distant.

"Yup. Rocks that don't fit in are called erratic. That's another word for irregular." I pulled another blade of grass and twirled it around my finger. "The glaciers stopped in Iowa, dropping whatever they were carrying when they melted." I paused. "These rocks are irregular, and they're everywhere."

Eugene stared at his shoes.

I untwirled the blade of grass. "Although that boulder isn't from here, it belongs here now."

Eugene stood there, motionless. Then he slowly slid his back down the boulder and sat on the ground by its base, his head on his knees, his arms wrapped around himself. The cool shadows from the granite rock fell over him, a different kind of blanket. Eugene sat like that for the longest time. I shifted uncomfortably; I wasn't sure what to do.

Suddenly he lifted his head. "Why?" he said to me.

I just stood there.

"Why?" he asked. His lips trembled slightly. He looked

at me like he wanted an answer. Like he would have given anything in the world for one real answer.

I sucked in my breath. I had no idea which "why" he was referring to. Did he mean why were his parents having a kid? Why his birth mom gave him away? Why she didn't try harder?

"I don't know," I said finally.

Eugene just kept shaking his head and hitting the ground softly with his fists. It seemed like a pretty big question, that "why," which might or might not be answered; that "why," which the granite boulder might have been asking too.

Then I got an idea. I found a pebble and walked over to him. "This is for you," I said, holding it out to him. Eugene looked up at me. "For your question." Then I went over to my burying place, dug a little hole, and put it in the ground. "This is where my worries are. My hopes. My questions, too." I covered up the pebble and patted the earth gently. "Now yours isn't alone."

Mom and Dad were out when I got back, but Grandpa was in his room, sitting on his bed. Staring out the window.

"Grandpa?" I asked.

He turned to me and his eyes softened. I liked how his eyes did that.

"Here are your tapes," I said, holding them out. "I liked the mento one the best for the music tapes. I really liked the ones of you and my parents and Bird, too, but I couldn't get through them all." That was the truth. Listening to the happiness in their voices, in Grandpa's and Bird's and even my parents'—for some reason, after a little while I just had to press the stop button.

Grandpa's lips went thin, like he was thinking about something really hard. Then he went over to a wooden box that a lamp was standing on, put the lamp on the floor, and turned the box around.

It wasn't a box. Well, it was and it wasn't. It was a hollow, wooden cube with a medium-size hole on one of the sides, and there were these metal things that poked over the hole like long fingers. Before I could say anything, Grandpa sat on top of it and gave a few slaps against the sides with his palms and plucked the metal things with his fingertips.

I nearly fainted when I realized what was going on.

Grandpa was a musician.

And he was making the same sounds and rhythms as—

"Was that *you* playing on those mento tapes?" I asked suddenly.

Grandpa grinned, a wide, proud grin that made his whole face light up. It vanished quickly, but I had seen it, rays of sunshine.

I sat on his bed and watched him pop those rhythms and pluck the metal bars. It was a hollow sound, vibrant, alive. And the faster he played, the more on fire it sounded.

"Did you used to sing, too?" I asked.

Grandpa nodded. But the smile left his eyes.

"How can you do all this but still don't *talk*?" I burst out.

He shook his head and silence filled the room. He stood up, sighed, and turned the instrument backward, until we saw only the back of it, until it was only a box once more. He put the lamp on top.

"No, Grandpa," I pleaded.

Grandpa shook his head again.

"You can at least play music. You don't have to talk for that," I said.

At that moment, the door slammed and my parents walked into the house. I don't know if it was because I had talked to Mrs. Bowers and let her know my mind, or because I talked to Eugene in a way that was helpful, or because I was talking to Grandpa and he was playing music where before there was only silence, but I felt like talking and talking and talking, and so I burst from his room and into the kitchen, where my parents were putting down grocery bags.

"Why doesn't Grandpa talk?" It was almost an accusation.

My parents froze. Then, after a moment, they seemed to come to life again. "What do you mean?" Dad asked cautiously. "You know why, Jewel. Bird died."

"Yes, but why is he still silent?" I said, putting my hands on my hips. "I mean, people die all the time, but that doesn't mean that the whole world doesn't talk. You can be sad for a while, but . . . why doesn't Grandpa talk?"

Dad jingled the coins in his pocket and started to walk away when Mom laughed. It was a hard laugh. "Oh, so she needs to know about the spirit world but not about the curse?" she asked.

My back muscles went tight. "There's a curse?"

"Tell her, Nigel. This must be a sign," Mom said mockingly.

"She doesn't need to know," Dad replied tightly. His back was still to us.

"Oh, you don't believe in signs now?" Mom pursed her lips triumphantly. "How convenient. You tell her or I will."

There was the longest pause. An awful pause.

Dad turned but didn't look at me. "Jewel, there's a curse on Grandpa's mouth for nicknaming him Bird."

I gasped. "Who put a curse on him?" I asked.

Dad looked back at Mom, then to me. He grimaced. "I did."

CHAPTER NINETEEN

"YOU *what*?" I asked. My hand went to my mouth.

"Jewel, it's not what it seems," Dad replied quickly. He took a step toward me, his arm outstretched. I took two steps away.

"Nigel, don't push her," Mom said.

I looked at him, then at Mom. Everything was coming undone. Mom's hair was escaping from her ponytail. Dad's black shoes were scuffed up. I sank onto the sofa and put my head in my hands. This couldn't be. Dad loved to tell me stories. He loved his garden and his music.

Dad cursed Grandpa. His own father. *Pooba.*

"It was an accident," Dad said.

I glared at him. "Really. Accidental curses. You never told me about those."

Dad flinched. Then he took a deep breath and yanked at the collar of his work shirt. "Jewel, Grandpa didn't believe in duppies."

"Really. And the rice? The rosemary?"

Dad sighed. "That was *after* Bird died. When it was too late." He was serious.

My head suddenly throbbed. Brains shouldn't get this overwhelmed.

"Nigel, don't torture her like this," Mom said. She crossed her arms. "Just tell her."

Dad jingled the coins in his pocket again. His eyes met mine, and I was startled to see how afraid they were. "When Grandpa and Granny came to the States, Grandpa didn't believe that duppies existed here," Dad said. "They don't cross water, Grandpa said. They can't leave Jamaica. If Americans think rosemary is only for eating, we need to do the same thing." Dad sat down next to me on the sofa, but it felt like an ocean of distance between us, awful and cold. "Americans don't protect themselves from duppies and nothing happens to them. Nothing will happen to us, either."

Dad took a coin out of his pocket and started rubbing it hard between his thumb and forefinger. I didn't know if that was to bring luck or just because he was nervous. "Granny was upset because Grandpa didn't take her warnings seriously."

Dad looked away. "Granny had been known in her village for making talismans. She knew about these things."

Talismans. Things to protect people from evil spirits. I realized right then and there how much I didn't know about Granny. Or anyone, really. I would never have guessed that Grandpa had been as skeptical as Mom, or that Dad could curse his own father.

"Grandpa kept insisting that things are different here," Dad continued, his voice hardening, "and even if there are duppies, they must have lost their power."

"But then Bird jumped," I whispered.

It made so much sense now. Of course Grandpa would be so sad—he practically dared a duppy to come. And of course he would be angry—at Dad, at himself. And that's why he was so attentive to things like duppies and rice and rosemary and Eugene, because he was trying to make up for what he'd done to Bird. He was trying to protect us so he wouldn't bring in another duppy.

"I found Bird," Dad said. His voice was thick.

"You did?" I asked. No one told me who found him first. No one really talked about that night.

"Grandpa was looking for Bird with me, and the moment I found my son I knew he was . . ." Dad looked away. "I was so upset at Grandpa that I did some things right there, horrible things. It wasn't a curse, it wasn't supposed to be a curse." Dad put his head in his hands, and his shoulders started to shake. "All I knew was my son was in my arms, and if it hadn't been for Grandpa, my son would still be alive."

"But how did you curse him?" I pressed. "Why can't you undo it?"

Dad shook his head. "I can't, Jewel."

"Why not?" I asked, my voice growing louder. "If you did it, then undo it."

"I tried. Granny tried." He looked at me with red eyes and shook his head. "I don't know how."

I stood up. "How could you have done this to Grandpa?"

"Jewel, don't shout," Mom said. Her face was long and tired.

Dad said nothing.

"How could you put on a curse and not know how to take it off?" I asked. Grandpa could probably hear every word from his room.

"I don't know, Jewel. But I lost my son that day."

You got a daughter, too, I wanted to scream. I pressed my fingernails into my palms until my hands were outright shrieking, then took a deep breath. I would have given anything to be in a space rocket with Eugene right then, careening away from everyone.

"Grandpa is a good person. Kind and interesting," I announced, glaring at Dad. "He didn't mean to kill Bird. And because of that, you put a curse on him that makes him go all silent, where he doesn't even want to cook or sing or play his instruments anymore because you've shut up his heart."

Dad stood up. "Jewel, I didn't mean it to be like this. Please. Try to understand."

But I wasn't done yet. "You tell me to respect my elders, but look at you."

His face was tight. "It's not what you think, Jewel—"

"You were right, Dad," I said.

"About what?"

I lifted my chin. "There are some things you can't forgive."

Mom looked at me for the longest time, her eyes glistening.

Grandpa was in his room. I burst in and threw my arms around him, and he hugged me back. I pulled away and peered at him. In Grandpa's face I could see that it was true. Every last word of it.

"But why?" I cried. "What can undo the curse?"

Grandpa shook his head.

I looked straight at him. "Grandpa, I want you to talk."

He swallowed hard, and his lips pressed together. *I know.*

"Talk, Grandpa." I took his hand and pressed it hard.

He squeezed my hand back.

It was then that I heard Mom and Dad starting to argue in the living room. Again.

I tried to ignore them. "I'm going to find what it takes to make you talk," I insisted to Grandpa. "Even if it is a curse. I'll find the solution. I will."

Grandpa sighed. Like he had given up.

That made me mad. "How come Bird got Pooba, and I don't get anything?"

His face broke right in front of me, but I didn't care anymore. It was true. I lost everything before I even had a chance to fight for it.

Grandpa walked to his window and looked out over our yard, turning so I couldn't see all the pain on his face. And somehow, even though we were in the very same room, it seemed like there was an ocean between us.

Anger rushed in my ears. "Grandpa, I—"

Dad's voice suddenly got louder. "Stop it, Rose. It was not my fault," he said.

"Oh, no? You let him run off," Mom retorted.

Something in the way they were talking made me freeze.

"I didn't 'let' him," Dad said testily.

"You were in the precious garden." Mom's voice climbed up the walls. "Didn't you know that kids need to be watched? I told you to keep watch!"

Grandpa looked deep into my eyes, his face wide with fear.

"It was a couple minutes," Dad said. "You're going to hold those couple minutes against me for the rest of my life?"

"Those couple minutes turned into hours, which turned into our *son's* life."

I stared back at Grandpa. They were talking about the night Bird jumped.

I shouldn't be listening to this, I realized. But I didn't leave Grandpa's room. I didn't stop them.

"You never told me that Granny went inside with you," Dad snapped back. "She had been playing with him."

"Oh, so I have to do everything here? Cook, clean, watch Bird, and have a baby by myself at the same time? How is that supposed to work out, Nigel? So you can stay in your garden and daydream about Jamaica?"

"If I had known you were going into labor, I wouldn't have been in the garden. You know that."

I could hear Dad cross the living room, with Mom following him.

"People don't plan to have babies, Nigel. Babies come

when they come. And if they're weeks early, then they're weeks early."

Grandpa came over and sat me down on his bed. Then he made as if to leave, to stop their fighting, but I held on to his arm. *Don't stop them. I need to know.*

"You could have at least told me something," Dad said. "Anything. How was I to know that Granny left Bird?"

"*Bird*," Mom spat. "I hate that name. His name is *John*, and I should have known better than to trust him with you!"

"You have no idea how hard we looked for him!" Dad sobbed suddenly, his words twisting high like a girl's. "Do you know how scared—"

"Do you think it's easy to be in labor when your son is missing?" Mom shrieked. "Do you think I wanted to be giving birth to Jewel? I didn't want Jewel! I wanted my son! Where is my son? My son . . . John, my son . . ."

Right then, my heart went numb. I felt nothing at all. If someone had dug into my chest with a rusty shovel, scooped out my heart, and bashed it in like a field mouse, I don't think I would have noticed.

I didn't want Jewel! I wanted my son!

I was never wanted. Not even the moment I was coming into the world.

I stood up from Grandpa's bed and slowly opened his

door. Mom was weeping into her folded arms, her head down on the kitchen table. Dad was by the door, putting on his shoes. I watched them. Even though I wasn't supposed to come early, I still did my part. I had tried so hard to make them happy. And they were supposed to want me and they didn't. They didn't follow through with their part.

They didn't even try.

Mom lifted her head. "Jewel?" she said, with a stunned look on her face. It was as if she had forgotten I existed.

I didn't respond. If my parents never wanted me to exist, then I was just a burden to them. I'd been wasting my time trying to please them. It had all been impossible and I didn't know it.

Until now.

Dad finished tying his laces.

Maybe if Dad didn't like gardening, he would have caught Bird and Bird wouldn't have jumped. I'd have a brother and I would be wanted. Maybe if Grandpa hadn't called him Bird, there wouldn't have been a duppy to whisper to Bird to jump off the cliff and Dad wouldn't have cursed him. Maybe Mom would have let Dad teach me about duppies and I would have stayed away from the cliff too.

Maybe I just didn't care anymore.

"Jewel?" That was Dad this time.

Bird and I really are a close binary system. He's a part of me. And Bird flew away. He didn't care what they thought either.

They were both watching me now.

"You didn't want me," I said slowly. "Neither of you did."

"Oh, Jewel," Mom said, her face flushing. "I didn't—"

"You just wanted Bird. Even though you got me that day too."

"Of course we wanted you, honey," Dad said. But he didn't move closer.

"Once Bird was gone, you gave up."

"You're misunderstanding things," Dad said, squaring his shoulders.

"What about me?" I asked.

"What do you mean?" Mom said.

"What about me?" I asked, louder. My parents stared at me like I was growing, filling up the room. Behind me, I heard Grandpa's footsteps approach. "Everything has to do with Bird. And he's dead."

Mom swallowed.

"Bird is dead."

"Jewel," Dad said.

"In the ground. Dead."

Mom shifted. "Now—"

"You threw my stones away," I said, and I was surprised that my voice didn't break. Instead it was strong. Firm. Cold. "You went to the cliff and threw my stones away. You didn't even try to understand," I said to them. "I hate you both."

"Jewel Campbell," Dad said, his voice rising, "you will not talk to us like—"

"You didn't even try to understand," I repeated, my hands clenching into fists. "You never wanted me. You don't have to pretend anymore."

Dad swallowed.

"I'm leaving," I announced, heading to the door.

"Jewel, we need to talk about this," Mom said.

"No," I said.

Dad put his hand on my shoulder. "Just sit down."

"Don't touch me!" I screamed, and I jumped back from him as if I were a wild animal.

Grandpa stepped to my side, his eyes blazing. He nodded his chin at the door. *I'll go with you.*

Silence.

Mom and Dad looked at each other for a long time, sending each other thoughts with their eyes.

"Be home by supper," Mom said. Her voice was heavy.

I stormed outside, Grandpa keeping up with me. He didn't

say anything, of course, but there wasn't really anything to say. What could he possibly have done? How could there be all this distance in a group of people who lived together under one roof?

I had never, ever felt so alone.

"It's not fair, Grandpa," I whispered.

He stopped then on the gravel road and hugged me right there, and in the way he hugged me I could tell he wanted to reach right into my heart and give it a tight squeeze, making the sadness drip out like dirty soap water from a sponge. The thing was, it didn't work.

I don't want someone's pity, I realized, my back muscles tightening up. Not even Grandpa's. In that awful instant, I knew I would never get what I wanted: I wanted them to understand how important the circle was, how special the cliff was, that I wanted to be a geologist and dig for arrowheads and be me.

But they wouldn't ever do that. Not even Grandpa. In fact, he'd be the first to stop me from going to the cliff.

A crevasse, wide and dark, opened up in my chest and oaths flowed from it: I don't care anymore about making people happy. I don't need anyone. From now on, I'm going to do what I want.

Grandpa suddenly stepped back from me. Eugene wasn't

too far away, walking toward us. Grandpa's jaw tightened, and I could almost see his great, feeling heart shut down, like that big hug he'd given me never happened. Grandpa would never accept Eugene. And that made me even angrier.

"Hey," I called to Eugene.

Grandpa grabbed my elbow.

I shot Grandpa a look. "Eugene's not a duppy, you know," I said, jerking my elbow away.

Eugene waved back awkwardly. And for the best friend that he is, Eugene would never accept Grandpa, either. Or understand how duppies ruined our life.

Grandpa's face was twisting up, mad.

The crevasse inside me grew, splitting open wider.

"Eugene is not a duppy," I said to Grandpa again, louder. I was sure Eugene could hear me.

"Hey, Jewel," Eugene called out. He stopped maybe ten paces away. "And Grandpa," he added tightly before turning back to me. "I was just wondering if you wanted to hang out."

Grandpa's eyes got squinty. He started pulling me away, down the road, back to our house. And I knew it was because he was trying to protect me and all, but I yanked my arm away for a second time and headed to Eugene. Grandpa hurried after me and tried to pull me, grabbing the top of my T-shirt, revealing the gold necklace chain beneath.

Grandpa gasped.

I spun on Grandpa. "Stop it!"

Eugene looked embarrassed. "I can come back later—"

"I'm sick of this!" I screamed at both of them.

I ran, my feet spinning toward the cliff. This was the cliff who saw Bird jump, who held my pebbles, gave me my stones, watched those stones fall. Like a magnet it pulled me there, and I raced to it like a bird flying home.

Eugene shot off after me, but I was faster this time. I tore off the road and cut through the cornfields. The rows of corn were taller than me now, hiding me, their dark and yet glowing tassels ready and ripe. They watched me burst from the fields and into the tall prairie grasses, heavy with seeds and eternity. My feet carried me like a vortex of wind, sweeping me onto the footpath and toward the cliff.

My lungs weren't working hard, not even strained. I nearly flew on the path, my feet light, barely touching. Eugene was behind me, his own feet grinding the tiny stones and twigs deeper into the earth. In no time, the footpath broke through to the cliff, and I sprinted past my pebbles and the gaping space where my circle of stones used to be.

I reached the boulder way before him. And the handholds were there, one after one, just as I knew they would be. My fingers became claws of steel, my feet became spikes, and I climbed up the rugged surface of the rock. It wouldn't be long now before Eugene would get to the cliff, I knew, and I climbed up faster than ever before. My powerful legs pushed me up, up, up, past the ledge where Eugene and I had sat; hand over hand I neared the safety point, the point after which the rock turned into smooth, worn skin and the handholds mere dimples, the point where I had always turned back.

But I wasn't going to turn back now. How could I? I was going to climb to the top of the boulder, and I didn't need Eugene's or anyone else's help. I didn't need anyone at all. And once I got to the top, I would fly, just like Bird. That would make Mom and Dad finally see me. And if they'd get sad and upset, it would be their fault. They threw my stones off the cliff, and my stones were a part of me, so why shouldn't I go too?

Eugene burst through to the cliff, leaping over my pebbles, dashing to the boulder. "Jewel!" he cried, propelling himself up the granite rock. "Please stop!"

There was no way I was going to stop. High above the safety point, the handholds were even worse than I thought, and the tips of my shoes scraped against the rock, trying to find purchase. But strangely, my fingers and forearms and legs weren't even tired yet—it was as if some tingling energy had infused my blood—and just the slightest indentation was enough to keep climbing, enough for me to throw my weight upon. I had never known this feeling before, this sense of absolute power and control over my destiny.

I was invincible.

Eugene had reached the sitting ledge by now and was frantically searching for the handholds I'd used. "Come on, Jewel!" Eugene shouted. "Don't do this!" I looked down to see his face all contorted, more frightened than I'd ever seen him before.

I didn't say anything. Not even Eugene was going to stop me.

Out of the corner of my eye, I saw Eugene lunge for a handhold—not the one I had used, not as good—and then stretch for his next one. "Go away!" I shouted down at him. Then I got a little wobbly and wrenched my eyes back to my own handholds. The top of the boulder was maybe twenty more feet up, and I knew Eugene was gaining on me. I was going to tell him that I had seen the path he was taking and it was going to get him stuck, but just then I found my next little dimple in the rock, the next slight curve to press the edge of my foot on, and looking just a bit farther I could see the faint path to get to the—

"Jewel!" Eugene screamed—a scream raw and primal.

My heart seized as I heard the slightest sound of fingers slipping. I looked back just in time to see the curve of his hands still stiff but this time holding on to nothing; I saw his eyes widen, huge and white against the black of his face, eyes of terror that fixed on mine, his mouth open in an O—

And then he fell backward, into the sky.

"*John!*" I shrieked, and it came from some deep, dark place.

His body seemed to hang in the air for a moment, so helpless, so about to be pulled down by gravity and forces and everything else that's out there that we can't see. And while he was hanging, suspended in the air, Grandpa broke through on the footpath, running, and saw the falling boy and heard me shouting "*John!*" and his mouth opened and this time a contorted, anguished animal squeal came from that throat. And then I watched Eugene fall. I watched his body fall through the sky and hit the ground at the base of the boulder.

And I heard Grandpa screaming.

I was screaming something too as I ran all the way to Mr. Williamson's place, the part-time paramedic, whose house was closest to the cliff, screaming something about *John* and *the cliff* and *fell*. I don't know why, but he stared at me for a long time—too long—like I was crazy, like John was already dead.

CHAPTER TWENTY

FINALLY, though, Mr. Williamson did move from his doorway, but only when I was able to sputter it out. "*Eugene*, not John." Then Mr. Williamson slapped his pockets like a madman, looking for his keys, and we hopped in his truck and raced to the cliff. He'd already called 911, but with the cliff being so far out, it would take them a while to get there.

He didn't look at me the whole time. Not once. His shoulders were hunched up to his ears.

My mouth couldn't stop moving. "And he didn't mean to fall, but I saw him fall and he's at the base of the boulder right now, and he was so scared and it's all my fault—" My breath was coming in short bursts, in and out, until I started to see sparkly lights at the corners of my vision.

"Jewel, breathe slower," Mr. Williamson said. "You're going to pass out if you don't watch it. I'll see what I can do." He was telling me this in his professional voice. Then he veered off County Line Road and plowed over the footpath. When we got there, Grandpa was bent over Eugene, knees on the earth. Eugene wasn't moving. Grandpa scrambled to his feet and ran to us.

Mr. Williamson hopped out of his truck and grabbed his first-aid kit from the backseat. "How far did he fall?" he asked me.

"Thirty feet," Grandpa said. His voice was a hoarse whisper, like a bad case of strep throat or maybe a rusty hinge, but there it was. His voice.

Mr. Williamson's eyes got big.

"From there," Grandpa continued, pointing to the place above the ledge. Grandpa stopped, watching Mr. Williamson watch him. "Well? Do something!"

Mr. Williamson ran over to Eugene, knelt on the ground with his bag, and leaned over him. My heart felt like it was going to explode. I looked at Mr. Williamson, who was getting out his tools, and at Grandpa, who was talking to the unconscious Eugene. *Talking.* And amid the awfulness, I laughed.

Looking back, I guess I could say that the curse on Grandpa's mouth was lifted that day, but why Dad couldn't lift it or Granny or me or even Grandpa himself, I'll never know. All I do know is that special things happen in special places, and sometimes mysteries are just that. But really, special places are everywhere. I think a place can be special simply because it *is*—it was special since the beginning of time and will be until the end, like the cliff—and other times a place can be special because of what we do when we're there.

Take the hospital, for instance. When the ambulance got Eugene to the hospital and the doctors rushed him away, Grandpa himself got on a guest phone and called Mom and Dad, telling them to come. Well, I think that just made the hospital a pretty special place, and that phone a pretty special phone.

For days Grandpa and I traveled the forty miles each way to wait for Eugene's collarbone to be fixed, along with his rib and his arm, and then for the X-rays so doctors could see everything on the inside. During the driving and waiting, while I can't say Grandpa was chatty, he certainly seemed like it considering he hadn't spoken a word in twelve years. Saying things like "How are you holding up, Jewel?" and "Want to bring out those dominoes?" Each time he spoke, his words grew stronger, more solid and anchored, like someone had wiped them off and found that beneath the thin layer of dust was a mountain of granite.

A good rain fell during those days, tapping at the windows of the waiting room. Mr. McLaren waited with us. He didn't say much and didn't sit that close, but given that I nearly killed his nephew, I couldn't blame him. Mr. McLaren checked on Eugene whenever he could, letting us know he was on the mend. Also, he said, Eugene's parents were on their way. There was a big storm out East that was holding up their flight, but they were coming.

I froze when Mr. McLaren told me that. What could I possibly say to Eugene's parents? That I had felt invincible and didn't think about their son, who almost died trying to save me? Shame wrapped itself around my heart, and the power I'd felt while climbing the boulder sputtered away.

That same afternoon the nurses decided Eugene could have visitors. It wasn't too exciting, though, because he mostly slept the entire time. Eugene looked so different in his hospital bed, so skinny and not strong at all. He couldn't even lift his head when he saw us.

It was hard to see him all weak and helpless because I knew for a fact Eugene wouldn't want anyone to see him like that. And it was even harder because I knew the only reason he got hurt was because he was trying to help me, to convince me to come back down. If I hadn't climbed up, none of this would have happened.

And strangely, even though he got hurt for me, *I* hurt everywhere, battered inside; even though Bird and I were a close binary system, I guess Eugene and I were too. I didn't think people could be close binary systems with more than one person, but maybe they can if they're really, really lucky. If folks have people around them like that, then no one would want to go off into space and never come back.

The next day in the waiting room, someone tapped me on the shoulder.

"Yes?" I asked, turning around.

It was Mr. McLaren, with two people standing next to him. The man's light brown hair fell over his glasses, like he needed a haircut but was too busy to notice. The woman, of course, was pregnant.

"Jewel," Mr. McLaren said, "these are Eugene's parents."

I stood up and took a deep breath. "Hello," I said politely. "Nice to meet you." I stuck out my hand, trying to be grown-up and all. Then to my horror, I burst into tears. How could I have done this to them? All I wanted was to be understood and yet I hurt everyone, disappointed everyone—if no one spoke to me ever again, I wouldn't blame them, not in a million years.

That's why I was surprised when I heard sniffling. I looked up at them and saw Eugene's mom brushing away her own tears. Eugene's dad's face was solemn. His back was stick straight.

"I'm so sorry," I whispered. "I didn't mean to."

They stood there awkwardly in front of me, and then to my surprise, Eugene's dad's shoulders caved in, and he started crying too. Eugene's mom hugged him, and they cried on each other for a long time.

Then, to my even greater surprise, Eugene's mom turned to me and included me in their hug, with Eugene's dad wrapping his big arms around us both. They had a funny smell to them, like a stuck-in-an-airport smell, which made me feel even worse. They had stopped their lives because of me.

"We were terrified when Tim called us," Eugene's dad said when we all pulled away. His voice was surprisingly deep for such a skinny guy.

I nodded mournfully. What could I say?

"We love Eugene so much," his mom added, her words still weepy. Her hand rested on her round belly.

I swallowed. "I'm sorry," I whispered again.

"You can't undo this, Jewel," his dad said, shaking his head. "We have to live with the mistakes we make." He paused.

"I'm sure you won't forget this for a long time."

I looked at my shoes. Not until the day I die.

His face softened. "But really, Jewel, we have to thank you."

I looked up, confused. "Thank me for what?"

His mom gave a sad smile. "We know Eugene's been having such a hard time. We really didn't know what to do anymore."

Eugene's dad shot her an embarrassed look and shoved his hands in his pockets in just the same way that Eugene would do. Then he seemed to recover and pushed his glasses back up his nose and took a deep breath. "Eugene's really changed this summer, and for the better." He shifted uncomfortably. "When we saw him just now, he could only ask about you." His lips twitched.

His mom nodded. "We've made mistakes too," she added, blushing. "You've been a very valuable friend, Jewel."

I studied the green flower designs on her shoes. His parents obviously didn't know those awful things I had shouted to Eugene when I found out about his name.

His dad cleared his throat. "And I must say, our son picked an intelligent young lady for a friend." I must have had a confused look on my face, because he added, "Eugene's told us about you. You're going to be a famous geologist one day, with all that knowledge in your head." He brushed his hair out of his eyes. "It's hard to impress our son."

A warmth filled me up from head to toe. I mean, Eugene said I'd make a great scientist, but I never thought he'd talk to his parents about me. I glanced at Grandpa; he looked proud too. Eugene's parents followed my gaze. "This is my grandpa," I said.

Eugene's mom tucked a blond curl behind her ear. "Jewel's a fine girl," she said.

"Good seeds turn into good trees," Grandpa said.

I'd never heard that expression before, but I liked it.

The night before Eugene was going to leave the hospital, we were hanging out in his hospital room, making the bed go up and down. "Hey, Jewel," Eugene said, "you want some of my meat loaf?" He poked at it with his fork.

"No," I replied. "It's too much like Mom's cooking."

He grinned, and I grinned too, until I remembered that Mom didn't cook anymore. Then I sighed.

Eugene studied my face. "You're thinking about your mom, right?"

I nodded.

"I knew it!" He smiled. "You see? I'm psychic."

"No," I said. "You're a—what's the name of the other star in a close binary system?"

Eugene's eyes got serious. "A companion star."

I snapped my fingers. "That's it. You're my companion star."

We listened to the humming of the machines, to the squeaking of the nurses' sneakers as they walked by. I was startled when Eugene grabbed my hand, but it was the kind of startle you get when you receive a gift you didn't expect. We sat there holding hands for a long time, connected like those stars.

But something bothered me, and I drew my hand back. "Eugene," I said quietly, "it's my fault you're here, you know."

Eugene looked away.

"If I hadn't climbed up the boulder, you wouldn't have followed me and none of this would have ever happened," I continued. "I was being stupid. You could have died." My throat tightened. "Every night since the accident, I've had awful nightmares."

Eugene opened his mouth to say something, but just then a nurse came in and checked his pulse, made some notes in a chart. I hated when the nurses came in; they talked to Eugene like he was a baby, like he wasn't supersmart or strong or daring. I was surprised Eugene didn't seem to mind.

After the nurse left, Eugene said quietly, "At first I was really upset at you. That was really dumb, what you did." He paused. "But you could have been the one to fall." Eugene's eyes were dark and full. "I'm glad you weren't." Then he looked away, and we both breathed a little easier. "Besides," he said, "you helped me realize something."

My brow furrowed. "What?"

"Maybe being an astronaut wouldn't be the best thing after all. I mean, wouldn't it get lonely?"

I grinned. "Nah, there's lots of rocks to talk to, from what I hear."

"Then maybe you should be the one to go up."

I laughed and shook my head. "Forget it. My family's got a thing with heights."

Eugene laughed until it started to hurt and we had to calm down. "What's today's date?" he asked.

I told him.

His face lit up—not like before, because he got tired easily, but still. "The Perseids. They start tonight."

I turned out the lights and ran to his window. I only had to watch for a couple minutes before I saw a streaming flash of light arc across the sky.

"Oh, my God!" I cried. It took my breath away, it was so beautiful.

"Did you see one?" Eugene asked, straining from his bed.

Before I could answer, I saw another. Then another. "And this is only the beginning," Eugene added. "The best time is in the middle of the night, when we're facing the forward side of the earth's rotation, plunging into space."

But believe you me, it is not easy to convince a nurse that two kids in a dark room by themselves are actually trying to watch a meteor shower—not until the nurse sees a meteor and gasps, and not *really* until Eugene starts spouting off the difference between meteors and comets does she believe us and let us watch the Perseids. Of course, it's still only with Eugene's parents' permission and then with the door open.

Grandpa seemed calmer around Eugene at the hospital—I'm not sure if he felt bad about being so mean or he realized that duppies can't have X-rays and decided he was wrong. Or maybe Grandpa realized that Eugene somehow had something to do with lifting his curse, so he can't be all that bad, even if he is a duppy: He might be one of those good ones. Whatever the reason, Grandpa was whistling when we got home that night the Perseids started, and he didn't even need to ask me if I wanted to, he already knew—we sat on the bumper of the Buick and watched those meteors careen through the sky, going from one infinity to another.

I slapped at a mosquito on my neck, but I was too late; it got me. I dug under my T-shirt and scratched.

Grandpa watched me scratch my neck, and he must have seen the necklace, because he nodded and said, "That's Granny's, you know."

When he saw the shock on my face, he added, "Granny wore it all the time. I put it behind her picture in the living room."

It must have fallen off when the picture fell.

"But why did you put it there?" I asked.

Grandpa's eyes crinkled. "I put it there," he said, rubbing his arm with his other hand, "so it could still be close to her."

Another meteor flashed through the sky. The night air anchored itself inside me.

"If it's Granny's . . . is it a talisman?" I asked.

Grandpa shrugged. "She said the necklace was for good luck, but I think she really wore it because it was beautiful." And the way he looked at me then, I knew he was telling me that it was beautiful on me, too.

I threw my arms around him and we watched the Perseids until our hearts were too full to take any more. Maybe it wasn't a coincidence I found that chain and good luck came my way, even though it didn't seem like it at first. Or maybe it was sheer chance and the necklace was just a necklace. The truth was, I didn't know anymore what was what, if it was coincidences or luck or duppies or spirits or God or other mysteries, but I did have the good sense to open my arms and say yes.

Even still, I was stunned when I found a glossy, hardcover geology book on my bed one day, featuring the major minerals, gems, and fossils of North America. It was beautiful. I gingerly hugged the book to my chest and was going to go to Grandpa's room to ask if he had given it to me when I saw my parents in the living room, sitting in silence, all peaceful.

I didn't have to ask them, and they didn't have to tell me.

"Thank you," I said.

Mom nodded. Dad's lips pressed together in a proud smile. "We thought you would like it," he said.

"I do," I said. Then my throat got tight. "But I can't keep it." I almost choked on my words. I extended the book back to them.

Mom cocked her head. "Why not?"

"We don't have the money for this. And I'm not interested in rocks anymore."

The room went silent. A different kind of silence.

How could I say that when I tried to be me, everything went wrong?

My parents looked at each other for a long time. Finally, Mom cleared her throat. "It was really hard to walk out of my job, to stand up to Mr. Robinson. But I knew that was the right thing. If I hid who I was, I'd never be able to live with myself." She shifted on the couch. "Do you understand what I'm saying?"

I nodded. My heart felt thick as I peered at her. There was still a heaviness in her eyes. She was still sad. But it was different this time.

"And then there are times to compromise." Mom nodded to a corner by the kitchen window. "Dad and I have been talking. That's where the coconut trees are going to be in the winter," she said. "If the saplings live through the season."

"Of course they'll make it," Dad said. The corners of his lips curved up, just how Grandpa's did. Then he cleared his throat. "And the cliff, Jewel."

I waited.

"The soil is pretty good over there."

I looked at him blankly.

"We can plant some rosemary bushes out there for you. To protect you." He rubbed his nose. "And I have some holy water. It's strong. Take it with you when you go."

It was then that I realized they still didn't understand about the cliff—maybe they never would—but they were trying. We were all trying.

And that had to be enough.

Grandpa was trying too, the way the kitchen suddenly filled to bursting with smells of curry and garlic and thyme. And he wouldn't let us help him—we would sit at the table, and he would serve us. He always served Dad first. It's funny all the things you can say the way you put down a plate in front of someone: You can say *I'm sorry* or *Let's start over* or *I love you*. Even though Grandpa was speaking now, for some things he still didn't need any words at all.

One evening after dinner, no one moved to clean up the table, which was strange. They just glanced at each other. I was going to stand up to clear the dishes, but Mom said quickly, "I'm so sorry you had to listen to Dad and me fight, Jewel." She fidgeted. "That was not meant for you to hear. When you're fighting and in a lot of pain, you can say a lot of things you don't mean."

I waited. Even though I was still mad at her and didn't want to understand, I realized that I kind of did. When I found out about Eugene's real name, I was in so much pain too that the words just ran out of my mouth. Maybe that's what Mom was talking about.

"When you're angry, you don't say things as clearly as you want." Mom looked away for a good long moment and exhaled, like she had an elephant on her chest. "What I meant to say, Jewel, was that I wish I had been giving birth to you without having to worry about Bird," Mom said. "Your coming into this world should have been one of the most joyful moments of my life." Her eyes got bleary.

I looked down and picked at a piece of dirt on the table.

Mom took a wobbly breath and sipped her coffee. "Nevertheless," she said, "it must have been awful to hear."

Mom looked at Dad, and Dad cleared his throat. "It's easy to forget about others when you're hurting," he said. He shifted in his chair. "We didn't mean to hurt you, Jewel. We've never meant to hurt you."

Grandpa brought out the cassette player that he was hiding on his lap and placed it on the table. He looked at me and smiled ever so slightly, then pressed the button.

My brain was all mushed up. Were they saying that I was right to be angry? Either way, I wanted bad to press that stop button because the last thing I wanted to hear was yet another happy time with them and Bird.

I was getting all worked up when the first words popped out of the cassette player.

"Hello, Jewel."

My jaw dropped. This was an old tape, with Mom's younger voice. How—?

"Hey, sweetie. This is your dad. How are you doing in there? Are you ready to come out?"

I looked at my parents, then to Grandpa. My bottom lip trembled. They were smiling at me across the table. I shifted my gaze back to the cassette player, my eyes glued to it as if my life depended on it.

"Nah, she's not coming out yet," said Grandpa's voice as the cassette rolled on. "She's still reading the newspaper, I bet, learning how to be a future president." A pause. "Hey, Jewel, we love you, and we're waiting for you, okay?"

My throat got thick. I could nearly see them crowding around the tape recorder, talking into the speaker. Just for me.

"You're going to love Grandpa's stew," Granny was saying. "You'll probably want it the day you come out. Forget about milk."

"Oh, Gloria, stop that," Grandpa said. "It's not that good."

"Stop being bashful. You know it is," Granny replied.

Then, a young voice: "You're gonna be my little sister."

I gasped.

"But remember that I'm gonna be your big brother and you're gonna have to do what I say," Bird said.

Everyone laughed.

"Oh, Bird," Mom said, "is that all you can tell her?"

"Hmmmm . . . ," Bird said, thinking. "No. We can play Superman. You can give me your ice cream. And you're gonna be my best friend. Forever."

Eugene's parents took him back to Virginia a couple weeks later. He was still moving really slow, and he was wrapped in casts and slings, but they made sure to get him a nice seat on the plane. And anyway, school was starting up for him soon. It was the night before he was to leave, and he was at my place, in the living room. I was drawing on his cast.

"Is that another flower you're drawing?" Eugene said, twisting his head, trying to see.

I smiled, grabbed a red marker, and continued drawing on the back of his arm.

Eugene groaned. "Look, I don't want to go to school plastered with flowers."

"I'm putting fangs on it. See?" I said.

"No, I can't see it, that's the point. I have no idea what you're drawing."

I grabbed a blue marker. "Then you'll have to use your fancy science to figure it out. Or just wait until the girls start talking."

The good thing about having your best friend in casts is he can't chase you very far.

But Eugene was in a different mood when his parents came by to pick him up. Everything was packed and ready to go home to the East Coast. Eugene shifted uncomfortably. "You really taught me something, you know that?"

"Like what?"

"I figured Iowa would suck. But there's a lot more here than I thought." His face got tight.

I thought I knew what he was trying to say, and that made me feel embarrassed for some reason. "Event Horizon is going to miss you," I said. "The boulder, too."

He nodded.

Then I got an idea, ran to my bedroom, and came back. I placed my rock collection in his hands.

"These are all my erratics," I said.

"Irregulars," he said.

I met his eyes. "Everywhere."

I wore his binoculars when we went with his family to the airport, and those binoculars crushed into my chest when he gave me the fiercest hug good-bye. I used those binoculars to watch Eugene in the sky as long as I could, to hold him in my vision until my eyes ached, until his plane dissolved into the blue, blue distance.

As we were driving back to Caledonia, I panicked when I felt the porcelain Xolo dog still in my pocket—I had planned on trying to give it to him, one more time. But then I realized that forgetting to give it to Eugene might not be a coincidence: Maybe the Xolo dog was really meant to be in the earth, just like how Eugene had thrown it there. Except it wouldn't belong to a pile of leaves. I'll bury my Xolo dog at the cliff, I thought, and that thought rang loud and clear. A strange calmness washed over me. I dug in my pocket and held the little dog in my hands. Its fierce face looked back at me, ready for anything.

"It looks like you're supposed to be close to Bird," I whispered to it, and then I had to smile. Because the Xoloitzcuintli dog protects against intruders and evil spirits, and it helps guide its master in the afterlife. Just in case Bird needed extra help finding his way home.

The truth was, losing Eugene a second time was like being hollowed out all over again. But this time was different. Stars in close binary systems are forever changed by their companion star, just like Bird changed me, and then Eugene, and Grandpa and probably people in the future, too, who I haven't even met yet. Or take Mrs. Jameson, even, who called Mom that very evening to let her know she needed help in the bakery and asked if Mom would want to work with her. They're not close binary systems, her and Mom, but it sure made a difference to Mom, with how happy and excited she was to have a job again. I'm sure Mrs. Jameson doesn't know a thing about Mom's cooking, or Reservation Chicken, and it'll be interesting to see what Mom will do with hot ovens and food, but I'm sure Mom can learn new things, or at least unlearn her old cooking in order to learn the new. It made me wonder just how much we're all connected, how we touch each other without even knowing it. And when we're lucky, we do.

I was thinking about this as I sat on our back porch with Grandpa, smelling of bug spray and eating ice cream that Mom got to celebrate her new job. Grandpa and I snuck some extra scoops after Mom and Dad went to bed. The Perseids were over, but they'll come again, Eugene had said. They always will.

"Grandpa?" I asked.

"Yes, Jewel," he said, digging into his ice cream with his spoon. I loved the way he said my name.

"What do you call that music box you played?" The

vanilla went down cold in my throat, stuck to the inside of my mouth.

"A rhumba box, mi love," he said. "Some call it a mento box." I also loved the way he sat next to me; our legs almost touched, and I could feel the warmth coming off his skin, making me feel all safe and warm myself, even with the cooling night air.

"And how old were you when you started singing?"

He laughed, and by now his laugh was smooth and creamy. "I sang practically coming out of the womb," he said. "My mom—your great-grandmother—said I was singing the night I was born."

"Really?"

Grandpa nodded.

Maybe it was because the moon was nearly full, watching us, that I suddenly felt brave. "Can you sing for me?" I asked tentatively.

And to my surprise, he did.

ACKNOWLEDGMENTS

I am standing on the shoulders of giants. These are the giants in my life:

Kathi Appelt, for the best hug in the world; Emily van Beek, the ideal agent; Namrata Tripathi, for her compassion and editorial insight, and who saw the vision for this book in its infancy; Emily Kokie, for her wisdom and support; Silvia Gomez, who patiently answered all my questions about Mexico and never tires of reminding me who I am; Stacy Jaffe, who was there at the beginning and read that very first story; Tom and Kristin Clowes, who have the secret-chapter-zombie-ending; H.T. Yao, whose unfailing support rallies me on; Father Michael Sparough, SJ, who stands guard; Zach Lulloff, who will get the first signed copy; Brian Ballantine, who let me miss his wedding so I could follow my dream; Brenda Rodriguez and Miriam Hernandez, the two girls who first captured my heart; Christine Brown and Barbara Nelson, who read the entire story and gave valuable feedback on Jamaica; and Keron Blair, who patiently fielded my plethora of Jamaica questions.

Additional thanks go to Timothy Smith, Kathy Kearns, Deb Sfetsios-Conover, Emma Ledbetter, the team at Simon & Schuster, Quinn Marksteiner, Bill Goldberg, Jennifer Newton, Esther Hershenhorn, Bob Raccuglia, Karen Bruno, Thomas Lynch, Amy Zajakowski-Uhll, Judith Ierulli, Erica Hornthal, Roseanne Lindsay, Gayle Rosengren, Darcy Pattison, and the community at St. Gertrude's Parish, who held me when I needed it most. Thanks to Molly Jaffa and Melissa Sarver, who found the passion in this book and multiplied it across the globe. To the librarians and staff at the Rogers Park branch of the Chicago Public Library, I thank you. Also, a special thanks goes to my family, for being the birthplace of all these stories. And finally, to God, the ineffable, the mysterious, the one who must be pursued.